Sue and Janet throw a sickie

by

Ade Annabel

First edition published in 2025 by Annabel Arts.

Cover artwork is by Jacqueline Annabel. Copyright © Jacqueline Annabel 2025.

A CIP catalogue record for this book is available from the British Library.

ISBN

978-0-9955922-2-3 (print)

978-0-9955922-3-0 (epub)

Chapter One

If you took Suzanne to meet your parents then, at the end of an slightly tense and dull evening, one of them would pull you aside as you went to get the coats and confide that, 'She seems like a nice young lady'. The word "nice", given generously and in all sincerity, would be doubly disappointing. It implied, as if you needed reminding, that, maybe, you had not turned out as nicely as your parents had hoped. Secondly Suzanne was, of course, a nice girl. No doubt about it. But that was probably the least interesting thing about her.

Suzanne and I first met through mutual friends in a red-bricked, Victorian house in Wolverhampton to the north west of Birmingham in England's West Midlands. It was at the end of a terraced row and had a large bay window on both of its two floors in generous high-ceilinged rooms. The whole house was larger and more labyrinthine than it appeared from the front as it went back from the road in an L shape around the rear of one of the neighbouring houses. The battered front door was painted dark purple but was bright blue in patches where the purple paint had flaked off. The front garden, if you could call it that, was dominated by a confluence of the street's recycling bins. To the left was a noisy, busy, new house infilled in a previous drive or garden during the Seventies. In front of the new house two children's bikes were laid or abandoned on their side with a few plastic toys, burst footballs and styrofoam containers discarded by passersby from the nearest takeaway. These had been thrown or blown behind a partially rebuilt Ford pickup with giant outsized tyres. To the right the next house in the terrace was boarded up with steel plates and covered in graffiti.

The room we were in was completely undecorated and so appeared large, blank, damp and vaguely institutional. I never found out who had rented the rooms or even if they had. I assumed it was chosen because it was cheap and convenient and must once have been quite posh in the financial ebb and flow of its neighbourhood. It was close to where I lived but not too close. The area had a bit of a rough reputation now although for what it was hard to say. You would just get a raised eyebrow or a funny look. So you ended up not telling people where you were going even though it was the sort of place where you probably should tell people or leave a note of exactly where you were going, how long you would be and who to contact in the event of your not returning.

Two small metal framed ex-hospital beds dominated the centre of the room but were never used, not even for seating as there were no mattresses on them. Opposite the entrance to the room there was a small door to an ante-room, lit by a narrow high internal window, which had presumably been used as a kind of walk in cupboard. Mark and Hugh usually sat huddled in there as they had found some cushions and blankets. I didn't ask them why they didn't take the bedding out and put it in the main room. They weren't very communicative and I found them a bit intimidating. In fact sometimes they kept the door closed and if you arrived late you wouldn't be quite sure who was there and who wasn't. The occasional lighting and relighting of Hugh's pipe was usually the only sound and smell to let you know they were there although they could hear us clearly enough. You would hear Hugh knock out the old burnt tobacco onto the windowsill before lighting it and taking a few asthmatic puffs. Nearer the large bay window in the main room the rest of us sat uncomfortably on old wooden dining chairs arranged in a semicircle around a filthy orange floor mat; more agitated than Mark and Hugh but equally attentive. At the epicentre was Suzanne who occupied *the chair*.

I suppose it was simply a chair. A worn, torn, old leather armchair, but at the time it seemed more important. Suzanne could have sat cross-legged on the mat but there was something about taking the chair that had an hypnotic or symbolic effect of amplifying our concentration like being called to the black chair of the TV quiz show Mastermind. The light from the uncurtained windows was behind it and seemed to glow either in the setting sun and then replaced by the sodium street lamps. It echoed the ancestral fire around which we cave dwellers gathered to hear the ancient tales. On the second night we were there the single naked light bulb, hanging from what looked like a toilet chain, blew when we tried to switch it on. No-one commented on it. No-one bothered to clamber past the rubbish in the long corridor leading up to the main room to find if another bulb could be found in the gas-smelling kitchen which was the only room that seemed to be stocked with personal possessions. Apparently other people were meant to live in the house but we never saw or heard them and never explored because most of the other rooms were locked. I assumed they were occupied by students and that they had left for the summer holidays.

Suzanne, being such a sensible nice young lady, as we've already mentioned, started at the beginning. She told us she was born in Birmingham. Mummy, in her words not ours, was simply a baby machine and dinner party host. She described her stiff hair set, permed and bleached into a beehive shape and the fact that she seemed to permanently wear an embroidered apron whether over her normal day clothes or formal evening dress when serving casseroles and profiteroles. Daddy was doing something dreadfully dull in "the city" that she didn't know quite what it was or felt was important. The city was just the centre of Birmingham not the UK financial centre in London so it wasn't necessarily banking or stock trading. Could have been anything office based.

"No Suzanne, your Daddy and I aren't rich – comfortable perhaps," she quoted in a ridiculously upper class voice. Whatever she said about her parents there was clearly some affection in her satirical portrayal of them. It didn't really matter. Suzanne wasn't spoiled and neither was she neglected or abused. I think it was the ordinariness of her background about which she was complaining. Only those children that have been spared a traumatic upbringing can complain about the mundane.

She was never a rich kid by attitude, whatever that entails. She went to a UK comprehensive school after it merged with the local grammar and, I dare say, she didn't notice the difference but she had picked up a slightly posh, and verbose, way of speaking, which at the time I found off-putting until I realised it was entirely genuine and just part of what she was. She bypassed her later childhood in her story; singling out only one incident in her early teens. We naively believed therefore that this must be important. It was, but not in quite the way we thought.

"When I was thirteen I discovered the consumer society. The part about consuming I understood very well. My mind was less able to grapple with the fine art of paying. In short, I would lift any item, large or small and do a runner. It didn't matter to me what. My bedroom soon became full of useless junk like a wedding present list gone wrong with multiple pop-up toasters and kettles."

"I've always imagined shoplifters wearing outsized macs with extra sewn-in pockets just raking the stuff off the shelves. In practice that never happens. It's too obvious. I limited myself to one item per store.

Although, of course, I wouldn't limit myself to one shop per trip. Sometimes I would pride myself on doing a whole street of consecutive shops. And not just big department stores that you could get lost in – though I did avoid some of the obviously difficult ones with high status glass cabinets like jewellery shops. I wasn't fussy about the type of goods, just the forbidden act and the challenge was enough. I remember taking a box of washers from a local hardware shop and later at home fingering each one individually and lovingly as I placed them in a row on my bedroom shelf. I loved the bright unsentimental and utilitarian shine of the metal more than any ring. I was just a magpie ... or call me a kleptomaniac if that's what "floats your boat"."

She went on to tell us that it started with clandestine sweet-eating as a child when she quickly ran out of her weekly budget set by her parents and wanted to find other means of feeding the habit. The sweets had gone but the habit had continued to develop to a manic extent. The fact that she might upset her parents probably continued to be a motivation although it didn't affect other aspects of her life or even her family relationships. There was no guilt, no self-consciousness, no deceit that affected her behaviour with anyone. She wouldn't steal from home or friends. Despite what she said I don't believe Suzanne was strongly motivated by the thrill of perversion, the sense of transgression or any enjoyment of a warped sense of arrogance in evading capture. Sure, something was missing in her life. Something she couldn't buy. She also admitted to an element of self-delusion when the inevitable fall came.

"I entertained no thoughts of being caught," she continued, "and in fact I never was. Not red-handed in the act."

"I often went *shopping* with a friend called Diane. From initially being much more timid than I was, she became over-ambitious,

9

stuffing objects of all shapes and sizes into her clothes. With a tight-fitting white nylon sweater and drainpipe jeans she could hardly afford any misplaced bulges. We went into Allenby's, our neighbourhood newsagent virtually on our back doorstep. Usually we went further into town but we had limited time on that day and decided to stay local. I think the distance from our everyday lives and the pull of the bright lights in the city centre normally helped to perpetuate our sense of invulnerability. Lifting for us, or at least for me, was some sort of fantasy fulfilment without any consequences or knowing the people you were stealing from. It was just big firms who could afford it. I don't know. I'm not sure we really thought about it in any meaningful way. But on this occasion I was uneasy about taking things from people I knew by name. I would normally be happy to chat with the shopkeeper whenever I went in for something and she knew me because we were on their paper round. So I hung back slightly and hesitated, looking awkward and wondering what to do. Out of the corner of my eye I could see Di stuffing a large old fashioned metal torch and half a rackful of magazines up her jumper. You could see the jumper starting to sag and stretch under the weight of the torch. God knows what else she had already taken and stowed up there."

"Mrs. Allenby was busy nattering to a wizened old man in a flat cap and raincoat. I thought their tones were low and vaguely conspiratorial but assumed it involved some over-the-garden-fence scandal. Di waddled to the counter pregnant with her spoils. Old Allenby took the money for the Love Hearts and Tip Tops that Di offered to buy. Everything seemed to have gone alright. Then suddenly the shopkeeper leaned forward and pulled at Di's clothes. "And what about these?" she thundered, triumphant. Down were flushed all the magazines, toy cars, a torch, felt-tip pens, batteries, sweets, a wad of envelopes, a roll of tape and, for a moment, I thought her breasts would follow. "We've been watching you all the time 'aven't we?" She throws a glance at the old codger, his head bobs like a toy dog in the back windscreen of a car as she continues. 'Proper little beggar aren't we, stuffing our jumper with hard earned...'"

"Mrs. Allenby wouldn't let Di go. She held her by the wrist across the counter and asked the old codger to lock the door. He was slow and I took the opportunity to slip past him almost knocking a woman and small child over outside as I stumbled through the door. As the door was closing I could hear Mrs. Allenby shout "I know you!" in a threatening way. She must have known I was with Di and my imagination ran riot as what might happen to Di ... and of course to me. I suspected that I hadn't heard the last of it and I was right."

"I never did learn properly what happened to Di. In any case it was during the Summer holidays and Di started at a different school after that and I didn't see her until a few years later, at a party. We didn't speak. We were incapable of anything but casting suspicious glances at each other above our separate companions' heads. I guess she blamed for something: even if it was just for not keeping in touch."

"I know Mrs. Allenby called the Police because I had one of his colleagues turn up at my house that evening but he never talked about Di and wouldn't answer my questions. To be honest I don't think he knew. It must have been a different shift by the time he turned up. In a more busy urban area nothing would have happened. The police probably wouldn't even attend and they certainly wouldn't follow up people that weren't directly involved but this was a sleepy little community at the time and they must have been bored or something. My father knew him to nod to in the street and perhaps he thought he owed it out of respect and deference to a pillar of the community or maybe he just wanted to rub my father's nose in it. Who knows?"

"Anyway the huge policeman breathed Woodbines into my face. I remember his long ginger moustache fluttering up and down with his stinking breath. I wasn't listening to what he was saying just to the way he was saying it and imagining his moustache was like a large orange and black butterfly I'd seen trapped in a hothouse. Men's facial hair used to terrify me as a youngster. None of my family grew it and the boys I met obviously didn't have it – although some of the girls had started complaining about stubble scratches. I thought facial hair was something rude and horribly adult. I could hardly bring myself to look at this man's upper lip and yet it continued to vibrate at the edge of my focus as I had to look down and stare at my shoes, feeling sick and thinking I was going to faint at any moment."

"He didn't shout at me. In fact I don't even think he really told me off but he did keep lecturing me and took bizarre pleasure in hinting at the frightening things that happened to women in jail. Then he roundly told my parents off as if they were small children. Again he didn't raise his voice but you could tell by their responses that they were finding it increasingly distressing, more than I had, as the policeman went on and on. After all the girl hadn't done anything, my father protested. Why should they be held accountable for what their daughter's friend got up to? For some reason the whole party ended up in my bedroom. My scalp was beginning to itch as my parents insisted I had nothing to hide, did I? If only they hadn't protested my innocence so much. I remained tight lipped of course, hoping that I would wake from this horrible dream into a bright Summer day... and just go shopping again. But that day wasn't going to come anytime soon."

"My chest of drawers, my cupboard, my desk drawer, the space under my bed. They slowly and reluctantly yielded to the rape of their treasures. I say slowly. The whole episode in my room with my parents probably lasted no more than two or three minutes but I seemed to watch it flow ineluctably in a hazy slow-motion."

I was startled as Phe suddenly sarcastically interjected, "So this is how you started on the long slippery slope?"

She had somehow broken the elegant web which Suzanne was weaving around her story and around us. None of us had previously questioned the poignancy of this revelation. Now, in the light of peer scrutiny, it seemed tame stuff. Teenage shoplifting was sordid perhaps, embarrassing certainly, but hardly the stuff of legend.

Suzanne, catching the sneering tone in Pheona's question, admitted, "Not exactly, no."

"Look Sue, you're not talking to psychoanalysts. This isn't therapy. If you want to make a point then make it and make it relevant." This voice was one of the rare cupboard utterances. Hugh I think. Suzanne spluttered.

Phe, sensing the group vultures were beginning to circle, tried to go back on herself.

"I didn't mean...well, you know. I'm glad you've told us. I just wondered where it connected."

Me? I was trying desperately to stay on the fence; and the pointed wooden stake of a picket fence is never the most comfortable of seats. I thought the cupboard was being obstinately literal about the whole proceedings. But I still felt too much of an outsider to criticise anybody. And anyway, knowing less about Suzanne than anyone, I was curious as to how this would play out. So I ventured a prod.

"Was this the first occasion you seriously questioned the ground rules of the so-called *capitalist society*?"

"So-called", that was good I thought. Hedging my bets as to where I might stand politically and making me sound more sophisticated.

"God no, you misunderstand!" Suzanne blurted.

Oh dear, I must have put my foot in it after all.

Suzanne continued, "I never questioned anything. It just happened. Thieves rarely work from ideological principle. Well, certainly in my case, there was no such motivation. Not even greed. And I wasn't taken to a doctor or therapist or anything like that. Look, perhaps things will be clearer if we leave it out for tonight and come back tomorrow?"

When Suzanne said, "things will become clearer", I anticipated murky depths for the following evening. But it had already been a tiring day at work. So it now seemed good to take this excuse to drift apart prematurely and unresolved. I felt the stiffness in my legs and buttocks from the wooden chair I'd been sitting on for the last hour and began to shift my weight restlessly from one foot to the other. I was a bit fed up to be honest. The whole thing had turned out to be something of an anti-climax to me. I had rushed to find this place like a breathless lover on a second date trying to make a one-night stand eke out into a meaningful relationship. I was intrigued by Suzanne and wanted to understand what we were supposed to be doing. But I wasn't emotionally involved. I wasn't invested in the outcome of anything she had to say.

In reality I had seen Suzanne before on the upper deck of the local bus and had already invented my own image of her life. In my version

Suzanne was the abused daughter of a millionaire entrepreneur who had been kept captive in a locked bedroom but who turned out to be the real inventor of whatever it was that fuelled his multi-million global business. It was a stupid fantasy. Just a way of passing an extremely boring rain-soaked commute. I used to stare at my fellow passengers and try to imagine what interesting lives they led. The young couple having their first argument because one of them had been seen in the chip shop queue with a rival. The old lady that was quietly disposing of her husband whose dismembered torso was in her enormous tartan fabric wheeled shopping bag. The leather jacketed punk whose nose ring got caught in the bus door when he got off and was dragged for miles. I was invariably wrong but I had high hopes for Suzanne.

In retrospect I realise I was going through a bit of dip in my life. I felt unusually nervous and vulnerable. Though perhaps I found the anxiety more interesting, even pleasurable, than any of my previous week's so-called pleasures. I just failed to take cognizance of it at first on that evening with Suzanne. I had been drinking, eating, going to parties and concerts with monotonous regularity. I think I had started to reach the point in my life where to stay in and work had become more enjoyable than to go out and try to force a sense of fun. But this was different...to be called at 12:30am at my flat in the centre, just as I was drinking the most revolting cup of Horlicks, and told to put on my shoes and coat, go to 109 Carver Road but park out of sight, knock at the back entrance and not to delay. Come right now. It was just a complete break from my monotonous existence. It felt like fun. I'm not sure what "fun" was. Still don't. But it didn't matter. I just needed a break. Something meaningful and, particularly, to get lost in someone else's world, through their thoughts and experiences, was a blessed relief.

I didn't know the place on Carver Road. I had never been in the area. What's more I didn't recognise the husky, thick, Guinness voice sliding towards me from the phone. Further enquiries were evaded. I was just told not to worry and that it was just a gathering of friends and like-minded people and all would become clear.

My first thought was that it was some sort of market research or maybe a financial scam like coercing people to invest their pension pot in a timeshare in Marbella. I suppose I should have ignored it and just gone to bed. I had, if not an exhausting day, then certainly a full one, both behind and ahead of me. However, because I was tired, the phone call took me curiously off-balance. It was that time of day when I tended to become smugly drowsy and self-centred, about to re-enter the womb of slumber. So I tossed the coin on chance and arrived bleary-eyed, feeling emotionally numb and not a little prone, as I took my place in the room passively and unquestioning.

Perhaps I was intoxicated by the coincidence of Suzanne's presence. She didn't recognise me of course. Maybe it was just the caffeine and the tiredness but I genuinely felt at first that it was the beginning of something new, something refreshingly different and that I was going to be changed by the experience.

Later, as I let myself back out into the wet, rain-darkened and early morning street, I dug myself deeply back into my Crombie, shrugged and imagined that I was already back in the womb, my womb, my room, tucked up in bed. It was a very comforting thought and the rain dripping from my nose was cosy. But you can't go back. Time doesn't work like that.

Chapter Two

What day is it today? Tuesday? Tuesday.

Work was hell. Sorry that makes it sound like it might have been interesting in some way. Work wasn't hell. More accurately it was purgatory. A long, so long, really long, period of numb blankness waiting for what? Judgement day? Is judgement day when you have paid your mortgage off or get the sack in the next round of redundancies?

I must have been scarcely halfway to the neo-Baroque monstrosity in which I made my contribution to society when I began to recall and replay elements of the previous evening's events. There was something about it that bugged me but I couldn't work out what it was. It felt like it was significant and yet nothing significant happened. I was no wiser at ten past five. Perhaps it was the absurdity of engaging with a bunch of strangers as if their lives really mattered to me that was troubling me. This sense of disconnection from my normal sense of living my life on the inside looking out contributed to a general failure to rationalise my working life. It wasn't a mental or physical tiredness but I guess what you would call ennui or boredom. If the truth be told I normally enjoyed the mind-numbing predictability of "the office" although, if asked, I would say I didn't. Work was satisfyingly secure. But that sense of missing out on something whilst caught in a never-ending sense of stasis was beginning to make me feel uncomfortable. I had a sense of imminent travel to an unknown destination. It wasn't good or bad, happy or sad. Whether it would turn out to be like a long planned, and relaxing, holiday leading to a change of lifestyle or a brief unpleasant trauma to challenge my complacency I couldn't tell.

Fine; whatever. Bring it on.

What really galled me, what really stuck in my craw, was my ignorance and impotence to arrest or speed my momentum or influence the direction.

I would attend the next meeting since it would surely be churlish to stand them up merely to prove I was a free agent. It would be like saying something hurtful to a friend or a relative knowing that you could get away with it and draw them back in and repair the damage anytime you wished. It was an abuse of freedom. In this rather fragile way I justified and cloaked the sense of compulsion that threatened to envelop me. Yet, when I finally found myself in the room, after measuring the surrounding streets in cigarettes, no-one greeted me when the rain started to get heavier and I had no better option that to go in and join them. No-one told me whether my presence was expected, necessary, desired. I was furious with myself and, of course, stayed as Suzanne was already in full flow.

"...and then there was no way I could renege, I mean, having wilfully provoked her I felt duty bound to follow her into the bedroom..." Suzanne picked her nose as she spoke with effortless elegance. Her white index finger was held absolutely straight as her wrist swivelled slowly, her continued confessional punctuated by flashes from her gilded bracelet. She was the first person I had ever met (I have since noticed it in others) who can perform the humblest and most embarrassing actions and gestures with such sophisticated assurance that it requires a high degree of self-control not to rush away to secretly practice in front of a mirror.

Suzanne was continuing, "She was slumped over the far end of the bed sobbing. Then she noticed me and swung around to shout me out. Her face was as bloodshot as her eyes and the front of her thick, dark brown curly hair was wet and bedraggled where it been pressed underneath her face."

Was she trying too hard to set the scene, I wondered? I suspected her description of this girl's "thick, dark brown curly hair" told us more about her than about whoever she was talking about. I found myself converting her bedroom scenario to my own purposes. In my imagination Suzanne was perched on the end of her chair and in distress. So much was clear. Her hair was blonde, almost white bordering on albino. Her eyes were not pink and pale. They were misty and blue. But she definitely had the panna cotta skin of a snow queen. Off white but without ruddy blemish or any hint of ill health. A thinnish oval face of stunning simplicity and symmetry. She wore a white cotton dress with light chocolate lapels and trimmings to the outsize pockets and buttons. Brown suede stilettos supported slim ankles and calves in light brown tights widening nicely where they disappeared. Her neck was framed with a subtle gold chain and pendant and I noticed, now I looked closer, that she had used her makeup very discreetly. There was something else. A scent. It may have been lily of the valley though my knowledge of perfume was almost non-existent. Whatever it was before it was now thoroughly mixed and mingled with homemade rollups and the background damp of an unaired bedsit. If I were to describe the scent it closely resembled now then the sensation of pressing one's nose up a civet's bottom would feature. But I'm sure that, with a sufficiently off the wall TV ad, with a breathy French voiceover, you could get away with it.

'For a moment I hesitated, drawing in a sharp, painful breath of air, then crossing the room in a single stride I slumped by her side, resting a good deal of weight on her back and bottom. Involuntarily I began to join in her crying. I expected her to resist, but instead she pulled me close. I began to feel what it must be like to be sneered at, and joked about, by people like me. The embrace became tender. More tender than I could ever expect from the pathetic ragbag of beefcakes and bully boys I used to call my boyfriends. Janet had stopped crying; and, as my breath came more easily, the tense knot of our bodies untwined. I too entered a state of drained inert blankness. After what must have been several minutes I suddenly started, and rushed, flushed, out of the room."

There was an embarrassed silence. Everybody embarked on a serious study of the carpet between their feet.

"Yes...?" Phe stuttered.

Suzanne swallowed hard. "Well...I...went back to the party. Robin, my boyfriend, was draped all over this Afro-Caribbean girl. I pretended not to notice and headed for the kitchen. I was pretty thirsty and was starting to feel the effect of too much cheap red wine. I didn't really know too many people there but it felt as though everybody was talking about me, whilst trying hard to ignore me. Once I had battled my way to where the drinks were stashed I had to settle for tap water. I drank this from a discarded lager can as it was the only container left (after I'd emptied and cleaned out the beer and ash cocktail within). Then I decided to walk out on the street for a breath of fresh carbon monoxide."

"Walking around the block was more tricky than usual (the pavement leaped up periodically to snare my feet) but it was a relief to leave the party. I searched for a quiet alley between the terraces to take a pee. That was good. Feeling better now. I was even contemplating walking home rather than depending on a lift from

Robin but as I was already approaching the house from the other direction I decided to face rather than duck the situation. Maybe it was something someone had said once about my getting a reputation for leaving parties without saying goodbye. Probably with less provocation than tonight. Anyway, the block or my walk must have been bigger than I thought as most people seemed to have left already – or at least nabbed a bedroom and closed the door. Then I remembered the shortage of anything even vaguely potable and the abrupt and unspectacular end that that can bring to the intake and outtake of various fluids. I searched in vain for Robin as, I was finally told by the host, he had done for me."

"Slowly sliding down the wall behind a cupboard in one of the less damp patches I felt a reluctant acceptance of the inevitable. Damnit Janet!"

"The camera panned over to the bedside table, the waves crashed upon the prostrate beach, the train whistled through the tunnel and the tall chimney was eventually extinguished and demolished. Only this time there was no power play, no phallic domination, no immediate distancing, relaxation and release expressed by a cigarette. Janet led me gently by the hand as a good Samaritan encountering a robbed and beaten traveller. Not as the foot-in-the-door cynic who must have preceded her. "Undress me", I pleaded. Silently she set about her task in a workman/nurse-like fashion. I began to giggle. At first she remained poker-faced, then a smile began to scratch away at the periphery of her pursed lips. 'C'mon you great lump,' she said as she brushed my forehead with an unmotherly kiss. Finally, finally, we managed somehow to co-ordinate ourselves sufficiently to pull the covers over our heads."

"Even at this stage we were slightly wary of each other. No matter how tired, how drunk, how desperate I might be I still found room for self-consciousness. I couldn't entirely let go. At first we lay slightly apart getting used to each other's smells – at least I was, and felt a slight gagging at cigarette butts, sweat, cheap roll-on deodorant and what might be salmon paste with a hint of somebody else's vomit. The combination threatened to engulf me but I was able to concentrate and relax into the body odour."

"Typical teenagers at parties tended to start with the face and work cautiously downwards, normally floundering round the breasts or buttocks where persuasion and resistance would be tested. So I worked up from the feet. Traditionally the smelliest part, but in this case a blessed relief from the rest of the sewage farm and quite odourless. I began to pummel her soles mercilessly but Janet turned out to be one of those intensely irritating individuals who are impervious to tickling so I shook her like a rag doll by the ankles. Then I tested her reflexes below the kneecap. If I could have found a rubber mallet I would have used it. But I became a little gentler as I began to knead her thighs. I embraced her around the waist, my head languishing on her abdomen. She stooped over and her lips burst on the crown of my head. I tell you this because I have never known such unpretentious tenderness, never such ease and simplicity, in the way we fell in love. There was no barrier between us, no need to perform, or aim for unwelcome slickness of ritual moves to climax. After all I may be no nun but I might as well have been. It wouldn't have made any difference. Janet would have understood and the experience would have been as intense and innocent."

It took us a few minutes to realise Suzanne had finished speaking. For all the joy she had encountered from this relationship there seemed to be an undercurrent of nostalgia, perhaps even pain and loss, behind her need to justify her emotions. To my ears there also seemed to be a rehearsed elaborateness and flowery stiffness in the way she expressed things. It was as if she were reciting a memoir that she had written down many years previously. I got the sense that she was setting the scene for a great disillusionment or some unfortunate event to follow as sure as night and day. Or maybe that was just our embarrassment that we had broken the lock and were secretly and furtively reading her teenage diary.

In any case we sat around for a while not knowing what to say. Or maybe that was just me and the dashing of any hopes I might have had of getting to know Suzanne as well as I might have hoped.

I looked out of the low window for distraction. The rushing rivers of brown city detritus had almost all been drained off the pavements. It had stopped raining. I noticed a filmy, filthy webbing of lacy gauze hanging from one of the abandoned curtain hooks higher up in the window. It was in delicate health but looked as though it would persevere after the glass had been broken, the frame flaked and the house itself brought to its knees.

Suzanne looked at her watch, but the rest of us were not impatient to leave.

Phe looked half asleep as though she had a huge debilitating curry resting contented snuggling up to her spine and filling her hollow legs. Physically she cut an impressive figure, half filling the room, partly because her features and girth were larger than life, but mostly because of her usually vivacious and engaging eyes. Now she slumbered; a beached and wistful whale.

I had briefly glimpsed Hugh tonight as he lunged out of the carpeted cupboard in search of a light for his brier. I might have known

– a deerstalker supressing enterprising tufts of ginger, somewhere in the middle of which could be discerned an old pair of round National Health-style spectacles and an air of self-conscious eccentricity.

Mark remained something of a mystery to me. As my mind wandered I began to imagine him as my caller and host, with a tweed jacket patched at the elbows, curly thin hair but with thick sideburns, buck or broken teeth with rolling bloodshot eyes.

Just as I was preparing to defend myself from the increasingly psychotic wraith, a pale young girl entered the room.

Suzanne leapt from her chair, rushed to the girl then hesitated. When it looked as if the girl might collapse Suzanne tentatively lead her over to the chair. As she approached, the first thing that struck me was that her head was bald giving her the appearance of a wrinkled old man. But surely she was no older than ourselves. She looked pale and harrowed, her neck muscles stretched and glistened with sweat.

"Er...I'd like you to meet...er...", Suzanne spluttered, "Janet."

The pale bundle was left in the chair, discarded like a jacket on a hot afternoon.

"Is she alright?" I wondered aloud, not addressing the question to the girl, in the same way that we talk about the very old or young in front of them, 'Does she take sugar?' I realised it was an absurd question, one that my roving eyes could adequately answer.

Then, for the first time, Suzanne addressed me by name, "John, you've been very patient with us. It's time you understood something."

"It certainly is," I ventured to interrupt but she continued over me.

"I don't know you and it wasn't my idea to involve somebody from outside. I don't know what you have been told but, for better or worse, you are now involved. I bet you were told it was some stupid truth or dare parlour game or thought it was part of a mock murder mystery theatrical experience in a hotel with very bad actors who couldn't get into the local panto. It was Mark who recommended you to us but personally, and I've got nothing against you *personally*, I wish you'd never come."

"Well thanks for explaining," I was sarcastically starting when Janet began to cough and wretch horribly. We all rushed to her except Suzanne. Janet was pulled on to the floor on her side and I tried to comfort her but was restrained by several arms. I pulled away in resentment and found myself staring into a face I felt I should recognise but couldn't for the life of me think from where. He turned away, and I left to the sound of unsuccessful vomiting.

Perhaps Suzanne was right, I felt involved. But the more I became involved the less I understood, and the less inclined I became to get further involved. They had treated me oddly or badly. There was no doubt in my mind about that. They had flouted all the rules. At first it was intriguing but all I felt now was a sickening sense of manipulation, of being duped.

While the others attended to Janet I left. Only Suzanne noticed but her expression was blank. I didn't slam the door. That would have been childish. But I didn't sneak out. I just left. I turned back in the direction of the traffic lights leading onto Carver Road. The shops were all boarded up – had been since my childhood. Now they had scaffolding and huge piles of sandbags affording them a temporary protection from vandals and graffiti artists and a flood of detritus. On a whim I switched on to the parallel residential road which gave me a view back in the direction I had come from to see if the others were also leaving. I suspected it was all some twisted show for my benefit but, if so, why were they treating me as some sort of outsider. I was exasperated but still curious and I was exasperated by my curiosity.

There was a dwarf wall on one corner where I could sit pretty much obscured by a set of dustbins and some large stinking, rotting cardboard boxes next to them. On closer examination the wall had some unpleasant sticky stuff on it – the residue of a child's chocolate ice cream or something similar. So I decided to stand or rather squat in one of the clean boxes. I tried not to touch the sides because I was pretty sure they would collapse as they had started to get a bit damp. I waited. The box wasn't entirely empty and I didn't want to know what was under my feet. I think it was just plain paper, polythene and some cut fabric ties. I must have looked pretty stupid to anyone coming up the street from the direction behind me but it was close to a cul-de-sac and it was empty at the moment. I waited. I waited a bit more. Then I got fed up or cramp or both. As I stood up, feeling foolish, I noticed a battered blue Ford Anglia back up to a gap between two sections of broken glass encrusted wall. A large thickset man in a National Coal Board donkey jacket prised himself out of the too small vehicle as Janet was being carried out of the building by Mark, Hugh and Phe. I resumed my previous posture. I couldn't see them anymore but I was close enough to hear them.

"Thank goodness! I thought she might come here," the man said.

"What the hell do you think you're doing? She almost ruined everything," Phe said.

"I let her get a breath of fresh air. I thought it might do her some good. She locked the door behind her and took off. It was really a gamble my coming here, just on the off chance."

The man's voice had a variety of undertones, some of which were rough and curiously familiar although I couldn't place the regional background. On the whole he came over as very refined and literate, but there was something else in there, bubbling under, when he was under stress which he appeared to be now.

They lifted Janet into the back seat hurriedly but delicately, as an ambulance worker might. And then I heard him go, car and all. I peeked out and the other three were standing, looking around aimlessly, so I had to squeeze lower, paying for my folly with a damp, and probably sticky, bottom. There was something at the bottom of the box after all. With relief I released I'd just got tangled in some adhesive tape and popped some bubble wrap. Holding my breath I could hear a few muffled lower voices now and then nothing. I dared a lightning peak and discovered that they were gone – either back in doors or off home. I couldn't tell.

As I straightened up and put weight on it the front of the cardboard box collapsed down both seams and I half fell forward onto the pavement. I didn't hang around to examine the contents now spread on the pavement but squidged through it, disentangled some trailing tape, and turned to retrace my steps back to the other road.

As I did so a matt black van of the type used for money deliveries passed me and drew up in the street. It struck me as odd because this was purely a residential area and there was also something else slightly out of place. Light just seemed to fall into it and there were no logos on the side or rear of the van. It wasn't shiny and reflective at all, no chrome trimmings and dark plastic on the unlit lights. It occurred to me it might be a bit dangerous for other road traffic on a dull day. A man got out. I couldn't see if he was looking at me because he had a crash helmet on. The visor was down and it also seemed made of a similar non-reflective black material but presumably was transparent from the inside like sunglasses.

It occurred that I might appear suspicious to anyone delivering money and, to be honest, I was a little scared by him. Anyway he seemed preoccupied by whatever information was coming over a hand held radio. So I made a dash around the corner and used a short cut through an alleyway. I figured it's probably not the done thing to skulk about behind bins watching people go about their business and, worse, possibly being observed doing it made me self-conscious and question why I had done it.

I preferred to think it was concern about Janet, perhaps mixed with a bit of anger about the others. Suzanne's apparent lack of empathy about how a total stranger would feel had offended me. I identified more with Janet – perhaps because they treated both of us as interfering. I had been prepared to be patient with Suzanne because the telling of her story was clearly some sort of personal confession, or the exorcising of some demons, so I was prepared to listen and see where it was going. But I was confused that she, and some of the rest of the group, didn't appear to expect me. Whatever agenda they had it wasn't the same as Suzanne. They rushed to Janet but simply to get her out of the way. Suzanne had initially helped her and then ignored her. Janet had become part of the human detritus that Suzanne was simply accumulating as part of her story. Where Di, and now Janet, had trod, I had the uncomfortable feeling my footprints would follow.

Chapter Three

"I hope he doesn't bring his fish and chips in again!"

"You're not kidding."

"The last time I thought he had raided Chris' aquarium: it wasn't much of a fish but boy did it stink!"

"Doesn't Boling have any control over his office boys?"

"Ha! Office boys, I like that."

Never had I felt quite so distanced from the neighbourly bitchery but I also needed it very badly. It was pathetic. A little attempt to restore routine boredom and disengaged faithlessness in which I felt comfortable.

I walked over to the window. I couldn't see a great deal, only the roofs we were supposed to clamber over in the event of a fire as there was no fire escape on this side of the building. The window we were supposed to open to get out was barred and the key to unlock the bars had been lost for several years. Salvation of computer data was given a little more care but even for that the fire would have to spread slowly in one particular direction, preferably downwards from the top of the building.

It was a miserable day I was glad to see. There is something comforting about the wildness of the squall observed from the warmer side of a glass pane. Pieces of autumn litter were gusting onto and over the roofs as the building was surrounded by what it considered prestigious gardens. They even named them The Cardon Street

Gardens – it was a barren handkerchief of tightly mown grass some thirty foot by twenty foot with one half-dead pollarded tree and a definitely dead tree stump in the centre which someone had tried to chainsaw-carve into a seat. Both were surrounded by iron railings and a locked gate. Presumably the only person who had a key was the person who cut the grass. In season it had three daffodils. Apparently, the semi-living tree had been one of a line of forty foot high copper beeches but they had got too large and the neighbours were frightened of them. Their roots fought the pavements for a while in heaving mischief but one by one they were felled for one reason or another. Most of them were removed when they used the space to put up another office block and called it, yes you guessed it, The Beeches.

I was waiting for an excuse, perhaps a change in the weather, to leave early for a prolonged lunch break. I wanted to perform the work task that I currently had perched provocatively on the corner of my desk by the waste bin in a single sitting and so couldn't concentrate on it just yet. As far as I was concerned I didn't have time before the public complaint of my stomach would become embarrassing. I had tried to read various documents and correspondence related to this task the boss had set but I was bored and would find myself reading the same passage again and again without realising it.

In this semi-comatose work/sleep mode I didn't notice that the Chief Executive Officer and section manager were in the connecting office and the door was slightly ajar. Through the glass screen they cast long glances in my direction but I figured that was because they hated each other and couldn't look each other in the eye. The Chief Executive Officer detested the section manager because of some sexual indiscretion with the section manager's wife. This was long before she married and had become a Director at another firm. But it gave the section manager an uncomfortable sense of nausea every time he met the Chief Executive Officer. Unfortunately this was coupled with straight old-fashioned fear and cringing subservience. For the Chief Executive Officer I think he felt some guilt (there was a rumour about how consensual it was) and he blamed the pair of them for not being forthright and able to speak their minds about anything – even the weather. He was always a very impatient man.

Still inside, I turned my jacket collar up and tried to sidle past their window. Silence. Whether they were talking about me, or just about something sensitive that I was not supposed to be party to, the frosty resentment was clearly not reserved just for each other. I tried to hurry past and even if they called me back I could pretend I didn't hear them. I was fortunate and rushed on down the stairs to avoid meeting any colleagues in the lift and having to make small talk.

The weather outside was worse than I expected but all I wanted to do was walk and dream.

Gradually, as I walked, the wind began to drop and the rain ease. A pale yellow light in the south brought a lighter shade of grey to the rest of the sky. I had got as far as one of the ring road roundabouts. I was surprised I had got so far on autopilot. In one direction I could see the first sign of weeds and wasteland that marked the brownfield perimeter of the city. There were a few warehouses and light industrial buildings but no houses apart from one derelict and boarded up terraced row where all the surrounding houses had been bulldozed.

I put my head down and gathered pace. I was headed for the empty fields beyond. I found myself overtaking a slowly passing outbound train that was dawdling past a series of red and amber signals. Or were they green?

I felt a sickening lurch in my stomach as I sped up even further. I should have bought some sandwiches. I could see Suzanne's face really close, nose to my nose, then she vanished as I was startled by a car horn from behind. I was in the middle of the road and quickly staggered back to the pavement. The car passed but there were people on the pavement just staring at me. I was just around the corner from where I worked at Harman Inc. It was still raining hard.

The people staring at me must have thought I was drunk, or stupid or both. I couldn't rationalise my experience and wasn't about to try. I thought immediately of the sessions with Suzanne and the other visitors to Carver Road. I was wondering why I merely wanted to drift along without attempting to take control of what was happening. It was all part of an increasing capacity I had noticed to drift off. I seemed to pass into a dream state in which the events or thoughts I experienced had no relation to reality. At least that's what I assumed. I would go to Carver Road tonight, early, and try and be more objective and rational. Maybe they were feeding me something in their so-called herbal teas.

When I got home that night I found myself experiencing the same breathless excitement that accompanied my previous visits, only this time I felt awake, really awake. I checked it out on a map and yes, Carver Road did exist and was mostly residential. I packed some ham and mayonnaise sandwiches and a hip flask in lieu of tea or dinner, although I might as well not have bothered. I wolfed it down within a quarter of a mile of leaving the house. I enjoyed the walk. I couldn't tell you what I was thinking about but just enjoyed the time and the exercise. Lately I had come to enjoy walking more and more as a time for reflection, to forget about work or things that needed to be done around the flat.

I arrived by cutting through an alleyway. Yes I had been here before. There was the rubbish still piled up on the corner. I could see the house and along one narrow side to a back yard. The yard was wet. Why do alleyways and shady back yards attract puddles and why can't you make out whether it is rainwater or some other black fluid like oil?

No-one about? Good. I went down the side of the L-shape to the rear of the house and there was a rotten wooden gate leading to an inner yard or, rather, a derelict garden space. It occurred to me how difficult it might be to get a grand piano in the back entrance. An absurd thought as no genuine signs of joy and music belonged in this place. There was a half-glazed door with frosted glass that seemed to be locked although I only tried the handle very gently, not wanting to make a noise. Then I decided to check the kitchen window as I seemed to remember somebody saying the catch was broken. I was turning my back sideways to the door when... Wham!

I slumped against the wall.

I tried to turn my head around only to see a black cosh making itself intimately acquainted with my nose. The cosh took up at least 80% of my vision but on the periphery I thought I glanced some Hell's Angel type with a black helmet. Only there was no insignia; no slogans; no art work. Just black.

I remember because I was trying to tell a fairly unimpressed police officer what to look for. "No, I've told you before. I didn't see his face. He was wearing a tinted visor which came down past his chin."

"Well sir, there have been quite a few attacks in this neighbourhood recently. I'm surprised a man of your background coming over here. What was it you said you were doing?"

"I was to meet a friend." I was about to mention Suzanne's name but said instead, "a bloke called Hugh, ginger hair, bit eccentric."

"You weren't trying to obtain…er…certain substances, were you sir?"

"Good Lord no!" Then I realised I had made the schoolboy error in understanding what he meant rather than looking dumb and asking him what he was talking about. If I replayed this conversation when in a calmer state of mind I would have looked at him in blankness and slowly repeated "certain substances, what substances?" I felt flushed and sticky with guilt even though I was innocent.

"It's just that there is no real way of telling who lives at that address, sir. It's a squat. High turnover. People without roots, so to speak. You understand what I'm saying?" He leered at me. I nodded gratuitously not having the slightest notion what he was trying to imply, but feeling it was probably to my detriment.

I left the police station forty minutes later somewhat discouraged and confused. I got my lukewarm tea and sympathy, eventually, after initially being treated like I was a criminal trying to get someone into trouble. I guess it was the best I could hope for. I was told there was insufficient evidence to justify any paperwork. I tried to leave my name and address should I be called upon to identify the culprits of any similar attack in which the police met with more success. I saw the sergeant screw the piece of paper upon which I had impressed my identity and let it trickle down the side of his uniform into the square, grey metal bin as I was turning to leave. Maybe I should have gone to Accident and Emergency at the local hospital. After all I had lost consciousness and didn't know how long I was out. Not long I suspect. At least they would have put me in triage, given me a bandage and a leaflet on looking out for the after-effects of head injuries. I might even have got two cups of tea or a coffee from the machine. But then again I'd probably need them in the time it would take to get around to me whilst there were more urgent cases ahead of me in the queue.

So instead I ordered a taxi and went straight home. With my "aggro-phobia" getting the better of me, I had the driver walk me up to my flat door and I tipped him rather too much. Inside the door there was a note on a small piece of paper which had fallen up against the white skirting board, camouflaging it from me. A cup of Horlicks is what I need now. What is it with hot drinks being the nearest thing the British can get to receiving emotional sympathy? I put on all the lights I could and selected Wagner's Ride of the Valkyries to play very loud on my media player even though it made my head throb again.

Slowly it dawned on me that the music had finished some time ago and that I was listening to silence. In any case the device had quickly gone on to playing totally unrelated music either at random or because the service genuinely believed that whatever pap it played was something I was bound to appreciate. What eventually grabbed my attention was it giving up and going into power save mode... at four o'clock in the morning. I switched it off and rather unnecessarily pulled the plug out of the wall, then fell into bed in the same shirt and boxer shorts I had worn all day.

I awoke fairly late and, after a shower, felt fully refreshed. The note blew away from the skirting board by the front door as if to grab my attention as I passed it to go out. I had fairly skipped out of the flat, as time was pressing, slipping the note I assumed was from a delivery man or meter-reader, into my pocket for reading later.

When I arrived the Chief Executive Officer and the section manager still seemed to be engaged in the same conversation. Not that I heard any of it of course. Ours is not to reason why, management moves in mysterious ways, we should just be grateful we have a job...all that.

I managed to submerge myself in something tedious, probably that task from the other day, and passed the rest of the day without really noticing it. Nevertheless I was contented. I had never really analysed it but the routine of going in and doing something, at least when my supervisor and super-keen Amanda in Accounts wasn't around, did result in a muted sense of satisfaction. When you had finished at the end of the day and the in tray was smaller than when you arrived, and nobody irritated you too much, then it was a good day. What's wrong with that?

Returning back to the start of my daily cycle was doubly appealing tonight. It was Thursday. On Thursday night I would go to the cinema or hang around El Congo disco bar in the forlorn hope of sexual encounters. Okay not that exciting then. In fact, I realised, it had been a while since I had left the house to do anything other than work, shop or go to Carver Road.

I remembered the note as I was rummaging through my pockets for my door keys. It turned out to be a personal note from somebody called "your friend MP" saying: "Welcome to the club! You will shortly receive notification of change of venue." There were several people with the initials MP at work but none were what I would call friends. Surely it can't be my local MP. I'm not even sure who that is but I can't imagine him or her dropping a hand-written note through the door. So I went through my phone contacts but that didn't give me any clues and I certainly couldn't remember any of them being into any sort of clubs. Mind you it could be Mark Sheppey. His middle name is Paul or Phil or something. He was the only one who was stupid enough to consider me a club goer.

I burnt the top of a frozen pizza for about two minutes and devoured it disinterestedly as I sunk into a comfortable amber armchair and waited for the evening to end. About a quarter to eight the telephone interrupted a fairly disgusting reverie. Fairly you understand, not extremely. That would be too exciting.

"Hello? 386032. Hello?"

"Listen. Next meet. City centre. 10:30. Back of the Odeon."

"Who is this? Mark?"

"Be prompt. If no-one there, leave. Don't hang about."

"Look, I don't feel like coming out tonight."

"I know. I'm sorry John. About the accident. I'm sorry about everything. But I think it best you came."

"Cruk," said the phone. A land line or a pay phone presumably to my land line which I rarely used. No call ID.

Well that was an invitation I could refuse. What accident? Presumably my tete-a-tete with cosh and wall.

I was not particularly keen to relive that experience and had maintained a certain amount of discretion at work about the source of the strawberry smear across my nose. An accident, yes, walked into a door. What a numpty. Nonetheless at the back of my mind a voice nagged and chastised me for being so stupid. A workmate, or even a group of my male work colleagues, wouldn't call me into the city to help my strawberry smear to recover from its self-pity. It would be a quick 'Oh dear' with a slightly glazed expression somewhere between confusion and concern and then quickly back to their favourite drink fuelled topics such as sport, office politics, boob-bouncing or willy-whanging.

No, when I thought about it, I was certain it wasn't Mark Sheppey on the phone. I think I had a pretty good idea who it was and what kind of experience awaited me if I was to go. Still, I was a little worried about Janet; a girl I knew next to nothing about and to whom my introduction was hardly conducive to... what? Friendship, empathy, giving help?

The buses had stopped for the evening. So I unlocked the bollards at the front of the garages and drove out from the flats. It was safer than walking and getting the bus anyway. I turned left along the slip road to join the fun seekers on the inner ring road. I refused several invitations to eat Joe's, to get down on Scamps' floor and finally to see what the Swedish Butler saw. I had to tour around a little but eventually found a side road where parking was unmonitored in the evening. A card in the house window said "Do not park here. Entrance in constant use." Perfect. I locked up and headed for the Odeon. I made a mental note of a late opening Fish and Chip shop should I be hungry on my return.

I checked my watch and slowed my pace, realising I still had a little time to kill. I must have been walking really fast. Round the back of the aging cinema the bright lights faded into an occluded neon drizzle.

Somebody had done their homework. The place was well suited in an almost B-Movie style to shady deals and back street trade. Not far from a well-lit main road where you could approach in a crowd and then quickly slip into dark corners. Sure enough as I checked my watch again I noticed a couple using the tall brick wall as a casting couch. Why here when they have a perfectly dark cinema where they could probably sneak in half way through a film and be warm and dry? As my eyes adjusted I could see further nooks and crannies in the alleyway which might well hide more crooks and nannies.

A woman approached me and put her hand on my shoulder.

"No thanks love", I protested but she persisted.

"Hello John," a gruff, very male, voice emanated from the now disembodied delicate lips.

"Oh my God. I thought you were a prostitute. I mean..."

"I've often thought that," he said, and a wry smile returned with his lips as I rebuilt my initial visual impression. Why I should think someone was female just because they had long hair (obviously a wig), lipstick and a funny walk I don't know. The light was poor but he looked like the ugliest drag queen I had ever seen.

"I know you, damn you!"

"Yes, well, we'll get around to that later. Listen. Were you followed?"

"What? Don't be ridiculous. I can't say I even bothered to look. If you want to hold my attention you're going to have to try harder than that. Was it you that bumped me about the other night? I bet it's the kind of thing you would do. And for fun at that."

"No, that's what I mean. Have you seen any black leather dudes with crash helmets and NO motorbike?"

"So it was you! You bastard!" I took a swing at him but as my arm raised it never came forward. Hugh was at my shoulder and locked my arms around me in restraint. I expected to get a stomach pummelling as I stood there defenceless. I looked into Hugh's eyes then to the other guy who I vaguely recognised as both of them were staring at me with all the aggression of a new-born gazelle. I thrashed a little and Hugh let me go. I was sullen and breathless as they seemed to exchange unintelligible glances, hand gestures and semaphores between themselves.

Hugh was the first to speak. "They closed down Carver Road. That's why we had to meet here. Probably for the last time. Altogether anyway."

"C'mon, what's all this 'they' business? Who are 'they'?" I asked.

"You mean you didn't recognise them? Your own security guards?" A pause. Then, in response to my look of total incomprehension, Mark added "Harman Inc. On the front desk. I'm Mark Patmore. I'm one of them but not one of them if you know what I mean."

My mind was reeling at the implications of the harmless computer-based entertainment and data firm where I worked sending squads of heavies or "bogeymen" to rough up undesirables in seedy areas of the city. Then Suzanne walked up to me from the alcove opposite. Her beefy snogging partner now visible in the neon light turned out to be Pheona. Suzanne glided in her normal elegant fashion until within hailing distance, then she hesitated, suddenly deciding to avoid my gaze.

"How's Janet?" I called. It sounded just as if I were asking after a relative who I knew was perfectly well. In fact I had intended it as a slightly barbed condemnation for whatever treatment they were giving her and the way they were treating me.

"Not too bad. She's not well enough to be here this evening, but she's getting better."

Whether she caught my drift or not I felt a little guilty. She obviously cared. But if so, why was Janet being kept against her will? If she had wanted to come this evening would they have let her?

"It's odd that you should ask after Janet." Suzanne said. "We want you to replace her. Is it alright if I sleep at your flat tonight?"

Of all the unexpected things that night that is the one that really took me aback. I tried my best to appear nonchalant, but the reality was that I was both curious and, although I hadn't really thought seriously about it, excited at the opportunity of spending more time with Suzanne no matter where that might lead.

But in my speech I was cautious. "I'm not quite sure what you want of me. I'm beginning to get the feeling that all this is some sort of industrial espionage to do with work. Do you want to get the right side of me so that I can steal company secrets for you? Well, I can tell you now, that most of our techniques and projects are endlessly publicised and overblown in the trade press. If there were any dark and sinister secrets at work I wouldn't be able to gain access to them anyway. Even attempting it I would doubtless be setting myself up for the same sort of pasting you reckon came from those security guards. If they work for Harman like you say which I doubt." I laughed, unconvincingly.

"No," said Suzanne. "Did we take you out for expensive lunches? Did we buy you little non-tax-deductible gifts? Did we send you copies of compromising photographs or hack your email or place large unexplained sums in your bank account?"

She waited for a reply. I was tempted to say, "no, worse luck" but as none was forthcoming she continued, "that's why I want to stay with you. We may not get another opportunity to talk as a group. Some of the others: Hugh, Phe and so on, don't know the whole story only part of it. I thought Carver Road would be a discreet and safe place although I appreciate that different people had different levels of understanding of why. I chose it because I thought it was the sort of place that no-one would bother checking. It was a squat occasionally used by students. A nameless, ownerless non-existent place. But Janet made a mistake. Then we thought you had too."

"It was our fault really." Suzanne continued after a pause. "We gambled on your inability to question or refuse orders. But we didn't gain your confidence properly first. It was a mistake not introducing you to somebody you knew and trusted from the outset. Someone to act as your buddy and convince you everything you heard or that happened was perfectly normal. We thought Mark could do it but he said that you had not really parted on the best of terms. He had to report you for parking illegally when you were late for a meeting and you blamed him for having to take the bus to work from then on. Plus I was determined to start from the beginning rather than in the middle, which made things a little mysterious and awkward for you. I think I enjoyed provoking you knowing that you wouldn't react badly."

"Anyway you started gallivanting around on your own and got yourself noticed by the wrong people. Your being an employee should slow things up a little, which is why I think we can still use your flat. We should make it look as though I am your new girlfriend. So in fact your little contretemps the other night has given us a viable alternative venue, albeit the others, particularly Janet, will have to go to ground."

I think my jaw must have been steadily dropping or at least fixing into some sort of grimace as I asked, "Why is it that whenever you open your mouth I'm less clear about anything when you've finished speaking than when you began?"

Suzanne gave a little snort. I noticed how relaxed and amused she felt. She made the most extraordinary things feel natural. "If it's any comfort," she said, "there is some element of truth in what you say. About Harman, that is, not me."

Chapter Four

It was a good job I remembered the fish and chip shop. Mutual munching of handheld Jumbo sausages naturally has a way of deflating portentous occasions or any awkward social barriers. I recommend it. Suzanne even insisted on entering the flat with me arm in arm and giggling. To be honest I was a bit bemused by it. It seemed theatrical, false and unnecessary to make us look so much like a couple. I don't think anyone was around to see us enter - either on the street or into the building.

I lived in what I considered an elegant flat. It ought to be for the humungous rental. It was convenient for work (a short drive or bus ride). It was straight on to a fairly busy road but there was off street parking through an old coaching-inn type entrance a bit further along the street. The building itself was a Georgian style red-brick frontage with a pediment over the old front door on the street (which no-one used now and was permanently locked.) I guess it must have been an office or a bank or something before it became residential. There were two bay windows at ground floor but I had one of the three upstairs flats reached by a side door that opened onto the central staircase. The windows and ceiling were slightly lower in the top floor but at least I didn't have anyone above me. The fellow occupants were young professionals. Very quiet. Very serious. No parties. One was Simon, a fair-haired bespectacled young man, who I think was studying law. He always wore a waistcoat and a badly tied floral tie over a stiff collar with which his Adam's apple lived in continual conflict. He had a soft voice and tended to speak in elaborate metaphors and riddles. The other was a young lady, Katy, who described herself as a coiffeur (hairdresser to you). She changed hair colour more often than her clothes which tended to be pink, crimson or white. She always wore jewellery, even for shopping or going down to the launderette, and had a dirty looking long-haired lap dog with no visible feet. I was pretty sure any pets were against the landlord's rules so she tended to keep him or her in the flat and it was pretty quiet except for when she was going out when there would be sudden yapping and anticipatory scratching at the door. She owned the salon where she worked. I know that because she kept telling me so even if we were just passing on the stairs. She would also ask me where I had been on holiday and what I was doing that day. I would tell her I hadn't got any holidays planned and that I was going to work whether or not that was true as it wasn't really the best place for a long conversation. I was always well whether I was feeling ill or not. Especially with Fido running up and down clearly desperate to do its business as my Mum used to say I didn't want to delay them. I suppose I was a bit snotty about Katy but I couldn't fault her for being friendly. If there was a fire I would knock on her door first and the lawyer could take his chances.

But neither neighbour was there when Suzanne and I entered the flat. I expected Suzanne to look around and ask for the grand tour. She just flopped on the couch. That reminded me to offer to sleep on the sofa. I felt the need to sort out the sleeping arrangements as a matter of top priority. She proceeded to give me a lecture on the hollow stereotypical fallacies of male chivalry starting with me opening the door for her.

I had the key so it seemed obvious to open the door for her. She was plainly not in a totally playful mood as she had pretended outside. So I told her that she could sleep on the sofa if she insisted. Fair's fair. If she wanted to swap at any time she could do so but I added rather awkwardly "not in the middle of the night I mean, but for the next night."

I couldn't really settle in bed knowing another living, breathing, snoring creature lay beyond the partition wall. My restless reveries and dreams were disturbed by a wraith-like figure with the face of Mark wrestling my hip out of joint.

More pleasantly I then imagined myself as a six foot rabbit surrounded by geisha girls laughing, drinking, playing soft lyrical music on the koto, having a game of chess, and holding forth on philosophy, religion and the art of correct tea drinking.

Then Mark entered. I managed to hurdle a row of bonsai trees and crash through a bamboo screen. I now found myself on a quay with old sailing junks lashed by ragged and frayed ropes tied to rusting, barnacle encrusted, iron rings. There was a steep arched stone bridge at one end of the quay. This is where Mark caught me. The fight seemed to drag on interminably. No punches or kicks – just endless muscle strain and the sense of being trapped under somebody's weight. I managed to climb over the side of the bridge wall but must have dislocated my hip in Mark's final grip as I twisted and fell into a fast-flowing current. I surfaced some way down stream then lost consciousness.

The next thing I remember was looking down on myself. Half my head seemed to be missing and my face was swathed in bandages. On the periphery of my vision I could vaguely determine the hooked beaks and bulging eyes of bird surgeons.

The dream then returned to a more pleasant, pastoral vein but I must have faded off into deeper sleep because I couldn't remember that part at all clearly when I awoke suddenly around six fifteen.

I tried to lie there still rather than getting up. I didn't want to wake my guest even though I was dying for a pee. After nearly a couple of hours I was just starting to drop off again when in waltzed Suzanne in a long, elegant pale green nightie (where had she kept that?) with a cheesy grin and a full cooked breakfast on a tray which she deposited painfully on the most sensitive part of my lap.

"Wakey-wakey! Rise and shine!" she chimed.

"Ougrmph", I replied.

I struggled to juggle the eggs, bacon and trimmings up to a suitable eating posture whilst simultaneously failing to manoeuvre my flaccid pillow into any kind of supporting role.

"C'mon dwaarling," she opined, "you've a fwightfully busy and important day at the office today".

"Mm...I'm beginning to think this might not be such a bad arrangement, little wifey. Did you sleep well?"

"Not bad. I found myself half under the coffee table about three thirty, but apart from that a relatively peaceful slumber."

"Mmumahubbayumyum. Aren't you having any?"

"I don't usually eat breakfast. But I did help myself to some of your Butter Crunch biscuits. About one and a half packets... so, I thought I'd cook you breakfast."

"Well, it's much appreciated."

She muttered something like, "first and last time" although I may have misheard as she had already turned and left the room. I was relieved in a way. I was not used to having women, other than a distant memory of my mother, serving me breakfast. Also, I was now really, really, really wanting to go to the toilet, but felt obliged to clean my plate and dress before crossing the living room. To complicate matters I had a huge and persistent erection. Caused no doubt by gravity and excess fluid rather than by Suzanne's presence.

Finally fed, watered, de-watered and generally spruced up I asked Suzanne where she worked. She said she had a job taking tickets at a local tourist attraction but that it was closed at the moment. In any case it was a next to nothing zero hours contract. She had got fed up and told them she was sick and didn't want any shifts at the moment. So I asked her how she planned spending the day.

"Oh I don't know. I'll just sit around and read I suppose. You do have books somewhere don't you?"

I ignored her. "We must have a serious talk about this when…"

"C'mon. It's the last day of the week. We can sort things out over the weekend. I don't want you to be late." She pouted.

"You really are getting too wifely – interrupting me in mid-sentence, nagging me. This won't do!" I mock protested as she picked up my car keys and politely ushered me to the door. "You've missed the bus."

"What? No peck on the cheek?"

"Piss off."

I suppose I should have been worried about leaving Suzanne in the flat but I had my wallet and all my bank cards. There wasn't anything really that was worth stealing. Just a few family knick-knacks that I would be sore to miss but I didn't think they would attract any attention even from a self-confessed kleptomaniac. As for electrical goods they were so old and worn I could do with claiming the insurance and replacing them.

I was a little late into work, but there were a few roadworks and a jack-knifed lorry which workmates helpfully suggested as the causes of my uncharacteristic slackness. In fact it had more to do with having to park half a mile away in the nearest and most expensive car park and then walk. All the closer spots were taken at that time of the morning and of course it took me extra time to drive around and check my usual parking spots. Frustratingly I could have made it in time if I had gone straight to the distant car park and walked. So I conscientiously worked an extra half of an hour in the evening and was just packing my briefcase when a fair-haired man in jeans and a black leather jacket came into the office.

"What are you doing here?" he gruffly demanded.

"I was about to ask you the same question," I replied rather feebly as an automatic response. I couldn't really have cared less who he was even if he was there to defecate in every litter bin in the building.

"It's after hours."

"Yes."

"Then why are you still here?" he asked, exasperated.

"I work here. What business is it of yours?"

"Yes, I know."

I was about to ask the question again but I just packed up my things and left. He watched over me like a broody mother hen. I watched him out of the corner of my eye.

"Goodnight then." I ventured.

He did not reply. On my way out I made a small detour to see Ken, one of the overnight security staff, who was almost, but not quite, friendly with our section of staff.

Well, we knew his name anyway and he seemed to know most of ours. He had recently retired from whatever he did before – I presumed the police force or some other public service. He was not in his office with the CCTV monitors so I hung around at reception for a little while. Then I saw him in one of the connecting antiseptic corridors swinging his huge collection of keys and singing some obscene ballad about Miss Kitty. I wondered why he had so many keys when most of the doors were electronic pass key entry controlled. They had probably just grown over the years and no-one knew which ones were no longer needed or could be bothered to take responsibility for the decision to dispose of them.

"Ken!" I called out.

"Oh, you fair startled me sir. What keeps you here at this time of night? Admin 4th floor isn't it?"

I didn't work in Admin but it was on the same floor. "Yes. There's a bloke up there in Admin. Asked me the same question. I was making up for time lost this from arriving late this morning."

"Ooh you shouldn't do that sir. We don't do flexitime here. You're supposed to schedule Timekeeping Anomalies for the following week's lunch hours. Although, between you and me sir, most don't bother. Not that I'd ever say anything against them sir, they've been very kind to me since the accident. I was quite lucky to find this job here."

"Yes, yes. But this bloke. I thought I'd better tell you about him. Blonde hair, jeans."

"Why? What about him?"

"Well, I've never seen him before and he didn't behave like a cleaner."

He looked non-plussed at me.

"Well I just thought I'd better tell you about him. Goodnight anyway."

"Goodnight. Don't you worry yourself about old Kenneth."

Doing good just does no good, I thought. People (I could feel a generalisation coming over me) are just not equipped to comprehend or deal with it. They think you must have some ulterior motive or, probably much worse, are expecting them to do their job properly.

I was looking forward to going back to the flat and seeing Suzanne. On a normal Friday night I would simply be relaxing in an easy chair with maybe a book or a television soap opera for company. This Friday night seemed more of a compulsion, an addiction, to resolve the situation with Suzanne… one way or another. But, on balance, it was a pleasant anticipation.

"Hello."

No answer, but Suzanne was there. I noticed sauce smeared plates tumbled with bread crusts and random books open and discarded on the floor. Two table lamps were on even though it was still bright light outside. A couple of half-filled cardboard boxes were in my chair. Suzanne's supine figure was recumbent on the couch. It amazed me how someone so meticulous in their own appearance could be so sloppy with a room.

"Mmrrgh?" she asked me.

"Certainly. One lump or two?"

"Oh, it's you."

"No it's the Scarlet Pimpernel."

I went to the bedroom and eased my feet out of my shoes. I tried all the muscles in my feet to see if they were still there and then lay resting on the bed. Yes, a hot bath would do nicely. I started upright as Suzanne leant into the doorway.

"Did you ask me if I wanted a cup of tea?" she asked.

"Not really," I had to admit.

"I would."

She turned and left. I relaxed back on the bed a little but then strained my body shape back to more closely resemble my Pleistocene ancestor homo erectus. I made a pot of tea and brought it into the living room on a tray with some biscuits. There were a few left although they were from previously opened packets and going a bit soft. Suzanne, to my surprise, was tidying up. Well, hiding the debris at least.

"What are you putting in the cardboard boxes?" I asked.

"Nothing. I'm taking stuff out of them. It's testimony. Hugh brought the stuff over this morning. I'd like you to read some of it later tonight or over the weekend. Hugh says Janet has escaped again; last seen heading for Wales on the Aberystwyth train. I don't suppose it matters now. She might be better off there. A bit of countryside, a bit of freedom, or maybe she's going to the Library there. Whatever, a spell away from us is what she needs."

"You've changed."

"In what way?"

"I thought Janet was like a demented, murderous half-sister that you had to keep caged in the attic for fear of what she might do or who she might talk to. Sugar?"

"No."

"No to sugar or no to Janet?"

"Sit down John."

"I'll sit down in my own home in my own good time, thank you very much." Then thrust the cup into her hands.

Suzanne looked weary and gave me that look I hadn't seen since my mother used to look at me when I had disappointed her yet again by failing to live up to the standards set by my brother and sister.

After a deep breath she sipped it and with an effort said, "It's a lovely cup of tea, thank you."

I sat down. There was silence...

Quite a lot of it.

I began to relax after a while and, I noticed, so did Suzanne. She finished her cup of tea. The soggy biscuits went untouched.

As much to break the silence as anything else I said, "I'm sorry, you were telling me about Janet." She wasn't but I thought it might encourage her to do so.

She spent a good while studying her hands and trying to find different ways of turning them to the light by the window then spoke very quietly, "It's true Janet is only half the person she used to be. She's no longer responsible for her actions. She tends to dream all the time. But I was never in favour of keeping her caged, like an animal. That was one of Mark's wonderfully humane little notions. So were you for that matter."

"I'm not interested in Mark. Tell me about Janet."

"After that party I moved in with her for a while. We became very close as lovers but not in a claustrophobic or demanding way. It just felt natural to spend our time together. It was equally natural when I later realised that Janet, or maybe any partner, wasn't what I really wanted. But I'm getting ahead of myself again. The reason I want you to know how much I loved her, and I suppose in some ways still do, is to enable you to understand the lengths I was prepared to go to in being absorbed into her life. I wanted to know everything about her. What she did at work, at play, in her sleep. You realise how difficult it is for me to explain or perhaps you don't. It just sounds like any other infatuation or crush. I suppose there was an element of worship. Anyway, I ascertained that Janet worked at a place called Harman Inc. and that she was not a scientist but it was the kind of work that was carried out in clinical conditions because she wore a white coat, which she was forever washing when it looked perfectly clean to me."

"As far as I could make out, from what she said, she would just stand around trying to make herself useful to all the other people who were creating computer graphics, running prototypes and analysing data. But it wasn't one of those small, start-up, young entrepreneur's type of businesses where everyone sat on sofas and wore jeans and t-shirts. It was set up much more like a research laboratory for a pharmaceutical firm. At first her job was pretty routine. She would arrange the transfer of text and images from the work output to storage media and check backups and so on. That often meant being first in or staying late; which were the only times that she was really busy. Unsurprisingly, she was eventually replaced by an automated process that was especially developed by her so-called colleagues to make her redundant."

"Now hang on," I interrupted, "you say Janet worked at Harman. Was that before my time? I don't remember seeing her."

"When did you join them?"

"About eighteen months ago."

"Yes she was there. That was about the time it started. They had a big local recruitment drive for administration. But you will know how little the technical staff associate with the rest of the company."

"That's something of an understatement. But I'm not really admin. I keep having to tell people that."

As the daylight was now visibly fading outside I became distracted by the orange neon flares from our old fashioned light-polluting streetlights and decided to draw the curtains. I wanted Suzanne to tell me more about Janet but I could afford to be patient. I had the whole weekend to cross-examine her. I switched on the standing lamp above my potted palm hoping it would provide the right atmosphere. Unfortunately all it did was highlight to me the sickly stunted nature of the palm, with cobwebs between it and the discoloured wallpaper.

Despite intermittent watering and cutting off dead leaves the potted palm refused to either grow or die. Why is it you only notice these things when somebody comes to visit? We think we are seeing it anew through their eyes when it is really our own adjusted priorities we are seeing. The guests are most likely completely oblivious to what is suddenly irking us and maybe they are disgusted by some other lack of good housekeeping that we had grown used to and thought looked perfectly okay. For some reason Suzanne was making me feel very much the bachelor boy although I felt that I kept the flat fairly tidy – almost obsessively tidy.

She continued. "Officially Janet still works there. They didn't make her totally redundant – they just kept reallocating her to train for other opportunities. First it was crappy retro pub or arcade games, then marketing film and toy spin offs from the main console games, then virtual reality therapy for specialist patients like Alzheimer sufferers."

"You've lost me again. As far as the Administration you think I work for is concerned all we see are video games and a bit of business software."

"I imagine the technical side of the business gets further ahead in research and development. So they are bound to be more wide ranging and advanced in what they are dealing with than you are. They keep everything confidential. Like car design. They develop some one-of concept car and keep it under wraps as it may or may not ever go into a production environment. They are probably three or four years ahead of you. The film spinoffs are probably still a couple of years from being made or released."

I looked sceptically at her. She knew I didn't believe a word of what she said about the company. After all why would she know more about the company that I worked for than I did. They didn't design and certainly not manufacture cars. I imagine she was just trying to illustrate what she meant by an example from another industry. Despite further questions she didn't offer any further argument or proof and that casual take it or leave it attitude, in a way, made it more convincing that there was an element of truth in what she said than her trying to offer repeated and reasoned argument.

"It's not important anyway. I'm not interested in Harman. It's the human side of it that concerns me."

"Well pardon me if I do interest myself in Harman just a little", I thought to myself.

She continued, "Janet ended up doing all sorts of odd jobs. They didn't want to make her redundant or maybe they didn't want her to walk out of the door with what she knew. I think also, because they had this recruitment drive going, I guess it would have played out badly in an industrial tribunal if they hadn't offered her some alternative work."

"Hang on," I objected, "I thought Harman was the villain of this piece. You're making them sound like a caring employer."

"No villains, just consequences."

That made me believe her a little more too. I expected her to adopt a high moral tone where she and Janet were the little guys fighting against the big bad evil corporation. The fact that even she didn't see things as that black and white was a relief. Harman had been pretty good to me... on the whole.

"Janet did some pool hours as a Personal Assistant and was shunted around from one overworked genius to another. She even helped out in the canteen when one of her friends dropped out to pick up her sick child from school."

"Oh the degradation!" I jested. "That reminds me I haven't eaten. Do you fancy going out for a meal?"

"Here I am telling you at last, and all you want to do is pig yourself at some Greek restaurant."

"Oh, I see you're one of those slimmers who believe in making other people suffer."

"You can eat as much as you want. I don't care. But I'd rather stay in if you don't mind. Otherwise you will learn nothing from me. We ought to stay in for the whole of this weekend and then you must decide whether you stay in work or we take a little holiday. I've bought a cooked chicken and one of those readymade Provençale sauces. I'll just do some veg and warm it up."

"Hang on. Step back. You're talking over my head again and I've no idea what you are on about. I can't possibly take a holiday at this time of year and at such short notice. I've already used most of my annual leave except for an odd day or two I was saving for some minor domestic emergency such as having to wait in to get the washing machine replumbed or some other maintenance or delivery or something I definitely needed to be here for."

Once again I was getting that giddy and sickening feeling of unwanted travel. I felt like I was sitting on an aeroplane, had briefly forgotten that I was sitting on an aeroplane, and then my body lurching as it sped down the runway into a steep incline in order to quickly grab an unexpected take off slot.

"John," she said simply, "sometimes you amaze me with your naivety and narrowness of vision."

End of conversation.

She simply walked away and into the kitchen.

I followed.

We cooked – sharing preparation in a workaday silence with nods, gestures and handing over of knives, peelers and saucepans. I didn't need to show her where anything was which made me think she had already checked every cupboard in the house and memorised the contents.

The meal was good. Better than I could have cooked. We laid it out on the dining room table which I rarely used and I had to clear off a few utility bills, gloves, keys and other bits and pieces that I'd casually deposited there because I couldn't be bothered to put them somewhere else. It wasn't candlelit. It wasn't actually a dining room, just the space in the lounge nearest the kitchen. Nothing elaborate. But it felt civilised and worth the effort rather than eating on plastic trays in front of the television. I suppose my bachelor lifestyle had encouraged a bit of lazy chauvinism or at least a kind of inflexible domestic idleness and routine with an over-reliance on the microwave and takeaways.

I didn't feel comfortable having my normal behaviour scrutinised and challenged like this. I tried to lead the conversation back to plans for the weekend, and beyond, but Suzanne seemed to want to postpone serious talk until tomorrow. Eventually, realising I was quite tired and being the wrong side of a few glasses of red wine, I begged leave to retire.

Chapter Five

I woke in a sweat. I had been having a lot of bad dreams lately. Sometimes they were connected by endless and tiring walking or running, sometimes they were quick physical jerks like falling off a cliff or more likely out of bed. My legs felt more tired when I got up than when I went to bed and the bedclothes being kicked around at the bottom would seem to indicate why.

This time I was sat bolt upright and through the light semi-transparent fawn coloured curtains I could see the faint red smokiness of streetlights trying to warm up a cold city fog.

I started to relax. Firstly because I realised I was no longer being chased by monsters or scary people. Secondly I realised I didn't have to go to work this morning.

But there was no chance of going back to sleep so I jumped up and began to dress. I crossed the sitting room, carefully tiptoeing past the slumbering pile of blankets on the couch, and then entered the bathroom. Washed, shaved and generally sorted out; this time it was my turn to present Suzanne with breakfast on a tray. As she struggled to get the sofa cushions to support her back, I couldn't help thinking that the condemned were going to eat a hearty meal. I just didn't know which of us was condemned or whether it was both of us.

"I like my bacon crispy," she said.

"What? So it flies off the plate when you try and cut it?"

"Yeah."

"Eggs over easy?"

"Which way is that?"

"To be honest I don't know. The opposite of sunny side up I guess."

We munched.

"Do you want any more toast, Suzanne?"

"Mm, please."

"About Janet," I started.

"Yeah."

"I was told Harman have a policy of not allowing staff to work in more than one department in a three-year period. The divisions get very uptight about poaching and internal transfers. How come Janet was swanning about from job to job? That doesn't sound right from my experience."

"That's what Janet said. She wondered herself why she was being passed from pillar to post. I think she always felt quite ambiguous about the company. It's not that I expected her to feel any deep loyalty … or animosity for that matter. I just think all that moving around made her very confused about why she was there and what it was all for. Personally I think that's why she took it. But I'm getting ahead of myself."

"Took what? What are you talking about?"

"The device."

"What device?"

"The thing she was working on. It wasn't unusual for engineers to take their work home. There was a fair bit of security around intellectual property and of course most of the equipment was simply too bulky or integrated to other fixed equipment. But Janet had started to work on what she called personal devices and mobility. That had become her new speciality as some of the older scientists could barely work out how to use a mobile phone, let alone something new. So naturally she had to take the stuff around for testing network connectivity in different locations. There was nothing unusual in that. Except they started to follow her around for some reason."

"So what was it? This device. Was it a mobile phone?"

"She never told me what it was. Like, I think, I might have said before I'm not really interested in the technical side, but I did pick up a small black thing out of her handbag once without knowing what it was. She'd asked me to fetch a Kleenex, or lipstick or something from her bag but, you know, old habits die hard. I never could resist shiny objects and took it without thinking, to examine it later. It was about the size of a mobile phone but didn't have a screen. It had some sockets. I suppose she attached headphones or wireless earbuds. I didn't notice at the time but I think there must have been some sort of camera lens set discretely on both sides of a pair of very fashionable sunglasses. Initially I just wondered why she had two phones and I guess I must have been having jealous thoughts. I worried it was some kind of burner for her to carry on an affair with someone else without my knowledge. In any case it's not important as I never really got the chance to examine it. I kept it for a few minutes only. Like I say, there was no screen and so no way to input a pin code or security on it so I just put it back. I assumed it was like an old fashioned MP3 music player with a simple play and scroll button. Maybe the controls were on the headcam thing which, of course, I had left in the bag. Really I am more concerned about the human side. I might have mentioned that. Anyway it was the affect it had on Janet and, in due course, on my relationship with Janet, that I want to talk about."

"Alright, what affect?"

"She started going for long walks. Sometimes she would run. Sometimes she would go swimming. She would go on trains, buses, boats... you name it. I didn't go with her but I would see her leave and I noticed there was often a black van with blocked out windows or someone on a motorcycle or just somebody walking. If it was on foot then I thought there was a team involved because I would see people signal by discreet pointing or nodding or lowering their chin and muttering into their clothing. I couldn't see a microphone but that's what it looked like. They were definitely talking."

"Maybe it was someone Janet was working with. You said she was testing connectivity. No great mystery if there was a team involved to do some kind of signal and response and check in with each other."

"Yes I suppose so."

Suzanne turned away from me and walked towards the big sash window. She looked into the street as if she was expecting to see people watching or driving past in a big black van. Whether she saw somebody or not, she went to the armchair and sat down. She folded her hands together, as if about to pray, and rested her nose down on the arch formed by her fingers.

Clearly I'd interrupted the flow of her thoughts again. I was beginning to read her body language and behaviour enough to know there was no point pressing her until she was ready to say more. So I busied myself with clearing the breakfast off the table and tidying up in the kitchen.

Ten or fifteen minutes later I re-entered the room with a fresh round of hot drinks. Suzanne was still pretty much in the same pose. I just put the steaming mug on a mat on the wooden stool by the chair and settled down on the sofa. Neither of us spoke.

I had a host of things I wanted to get on with this weekend. But it didn't seem polite to do any of them. Even if they were things I could have done quietly in the same room. So we sat in silence save for the odd slurping noise and the normally inaudible impact of a cup being put down to rest.

We must have sat like that for the best part of an hour when she suddenly piped up, "Mark was a security guard."

By this time I'd lost all sense of what she was on about. I had no context for this.

"You mean he worked at Harman or he was just a career security professional?"

"He worked at Harman."

"I thought he was familiar but I couldn't remember where I had seen him before. Sometimes I get confused between people I've seen on TV and think I know them. It's really embarrassing when you pass them in the street and don't know whether they will be insulted if you don't say hello because they are your long-lost cousin or old schoolfriend and then they turn out to be the newsreader or weather presenter on local TV. Mind you when I saw him face to face at the cinema I think the penny was starting to drop that he wasn't a celebrity."

"Typical. The security guards remember everybody and know most of your names. But they are just a uniform to you. Someone to walk past or ask directions."

"I do know some of the security guards by name and I generally speak to them even if the exchange is pretty limited to stating the obvious about the fact that it is morning and whether it is raining or sunny. It's just some of them are more friendly than others I guess. As for me I usually have somewhere to be 10 minutes ago so I'm not going to stop and ask them what they had for dinner last night. But you are right; I don't really make eye contact whereas they probably look you up and down. It's part of their job. I'm usually too busy concentrating on finding my pass and negotiating one way doors, barriers and lifts without looking like a numpty."

"I was thinking about what you said. That Janet may have been working with the people who were following her. I hadn't thought about it before but Mark might have been one of them."

"But you said she was doing some technical testing. They wouldn't have a security guard for that."

"Why not? Particularly if they were worried about intellectual property being stolen."

"I guess so but my first thought for foiling industrial espionage wouldn't be to hire a glorified receptionist which is all they are at Harman."

"There you go again. You have no idea of what work they do. Not a clue."

"Enlighten me then?"

"I don't either. I just don't like your lazy assumptions. I'm sure checking in visitors is just part of it."

"Yes," she continued, this time to herself, "that's it. Mark must have followed her and intervened."

I just sat and looked at her in silence. There didn't seem to be any further information forthcoming. I realised that Suzanne couldn't just come out and tell me what was going on ...because she didn't know. She was trying to work it out. I had thought she had some master plan but she was plainly winging it.

I got up and walked to the window. Without really thinking about it I glanced up and down the street to see if there was anybody watching or just standing around. There was occasional traffic but no-one I could see in the line of parked cars. There was a woman in a blue overcoat and a large 70s afro hairstyle trying to take the hand of a small child who was not wanting to walk. There was a pale scrawny man in his twenties or thirties in floppy grey track suit bottoms and a hoody who looked suspicious enough but he was talking on a mobile phone and pacing up and down throwing his free arm in the air and at one point thumping a tree. I didn't know much about spying but I reckoned the woman would be making a better job of keeping the place under observation. Of course they could have been working together.

"Would you like to go out for a walk?" I suggested.

"No I don't think that would be a good idea. Unless we ask Mark to shadow us. That might resolve one or two things. Let me have a word with him."

Suzanne picked up a phone and went into another room. I continued to look out of the window. The grey man seemed to be getting more and more agitated. The mother or child carer had gone. There was a couple of young women walking arm in arm down our side of the road. They were laughing and bumping into each other. I watched them go – envious of their life. I imagined they worked hard and then got paralytic on a Friday night. Simple pleasures. No regrets. Everything to look forward to.

I could hear Suzanne talking in the other room but I couldn't make out what she was saying. Something about Hugh, something about Janet but not much. Eventually the conversation sounded like it was starting to wind down to a close. I could make out one or two small sentences. "Right", "See you then", "Okay", "We will."

She came back in. "We'll have to wait an hour. They have to set up one or two precautions. I didn't think to ask you where you wanted to go which I should have done."

"You make it sound like a military operation. I was only thinking of going up to the park and back. Maybe go down to the canal if you really wanted to stretch your legs."

"We'll see."

I didn't but had no choice. "Another cup of tea?"

It was a cloudy day, a bit windy but fairly mild. Suzanne got a text when Mark was ready. She grabbed a coat and shoes (cursing the fact that she hadn't brought trainers although the shoes she had were flat and sensible – perfectly okay for street walking, paths and grass if not great for hiking or crossing a swamp.)

"One word of advice John. Don't look around. Just walk ahead perfectly normally."

"I normally do walk normally," I replied as we pulled the door to and skittered down the short flight of stairs to street level.

It wouldn't have made any difference if I had been looking around for Mark. He is one of those people that are difficult to describe and impossible to pick out in a line-up from a single sighting. Average height. Average weight. Average build. Average age, thirties or forties. His hair is dark with a side parting. I'd say he had a strong nose although I don't know what a weak nose looks like. The colour of his eyes are probably dark. I never really held his gaze. He would look at me intently, call me by name, be really friendly, but in a persistent and annoying way that made you want to only glance and move on.

Hugh on the other hand stood out in a crowd. He had curly overgrown hair, glasses, a fat nose, bulbous at the end, and not exactly buck teeth but his teeth were prominent, if only because he always seemed to be smiling inanely. He was too young to look like a mad professor, but it would be a good career option for later life.

We walked up in the direction of the Edgbaston then took an arching curve towards the old botanical garden. Suzanne seemed tense and not very chatty but as we got closer to the park, university and hospital she seemed to relax and make odd remarks about the street furniture, the weather, people we passed.

I was finding it difficult not to look around simply because I had been told not to. Occasionally I would make an excuse to turn and face Suzanne. She was irritated by this initially but the longer we went on the less she cared. When we got to the park I was quite keen to just sit on a bench and take a break but Suzanne suddenly became playful.

"Let's run," she said. She started running and before I could answer, and like a lovesick fool, I followed. I expected a quick sprint and a collapse into giggles but bugger me she kept on going. Her blonde hair was flying in the wind. According to gender stereotypes I would say that she ran like a girl. In other words she had an exaggerated rotation of the ankle encouraged by the bone structure of her hips that would have been ironed out if she had ever spent any time working as an athlete or sprinter. But I still couldn't keep up. Too much pizza and indolence. That's when I noticed a couple, one male, one female, in black tracksuits jogging on the other side of the park. They couldn't help but get ahead of me as I started to fall off the pace. They weren't particularly close but I noticed the woman kept her eyes firmly on Suzanne changing her speed up and down as Suzanne rounded a stand of trees.

"Where was Mark, the bastard?" I muttered not quite under my breath. Maybe he was the guy in the tracksuit but then I saw him or thought I saw someone looking like Mark duck down behind a bush about a hundred yards behind me.

Suzanne, seeing I was lagging seriously behind, stopped. She turned to face me and doubled up. I thought she was catching her breath. Then she just crumpled and fell on the path. A concerned lady dog walker rushed up to her and bent over her to turn her face and shoulders skywards. I started to run for real – not that there was anything I could do. The jogging couple were quite close now as we were reaching the edge of the park where the paths converge. The little rat like dog barked and barked like it was all terrific fun.

Once again, "where was Mark, the bastard?"

He got there before me just as the jogging couple went straight by barely even looking at the prone Suzanne now spread-eagled half on the grass, half on the path. Mark suddenly slowed and walked up quite casually to the dog walker. I couldn't hear what was said but he was obviously advising her to put Suzanne on her side in a more traditional recovery position (to stop her choking on her own vomit) and generally taking over.

I slowed down too and tried to approach at a casual walk but it was more of stuttering bunny hop. "Is she alright?"

Mark ignored me but the elderly lady reassured me that the gentleman had said she would be fine. I wondered what to do – whether to speak directly to Mark or play out some sort of charade of anonymity. But first I looked Suzanne in the face. As best I could anyway. Her eyes were closed and her breathing was shallow; both of which surprised me. I was still out of breath even though I'd more or less walked the last few yards. Finally Mark looked up at me from where he was crouched by her and said, "She has a medical condition which makes her zone out but she'll be fine in a few minutes. I can wait with her and make sure she's alright if you want."

I was going to ask 'what medical condition?' But I still wasn't sure whether we were pretending not to know each other or Suzanne or what. So I just stood there.

I decided to be cautious in the end and mumbled some apology about having to be somewhere. I wanted to do something useful and thought I should go to the edge of the park and see if the jogging couple were still around anywhere. I couldn't see them. Eventually the dog got too impatient waiting for the dog owner to walk on and she must have made her apologies and left. A few passers-by slowed and asked what was going on but not as many as you would hope for a vulnerable woman collapsed in a public park with a man crouched over her. Most hurried by or even turned around to give them a totally theatrical wide berth of several hundred yards.

After about 5 to 10 minutes, I wasn't really counting, Suzanne was sitting upright. She seemed to be very groggy but was soon mobile enough to be assisted by Mark and another passer-by (should have been me) to the nearest bench. I looked around again out of the park gate and there was one of the joggers tucking into some sort of power shake drink in a carton. She saw me looking at her. So much for my subterfuge – I'd have been less suspicious if I'd just stayed with Suzanne. I walked straight at her and then brushed past. She was smaller than I thought. Jet black hair tied back. Slightly Asiatic looking. She didn't react to me or even look at me.

I wanted to see where the other jogger was. I casually looked into the shops and alleyways around. I saw no café or street vendor where the female jogger could have bought her drink and I couldn't see her companion. When I turned around I couldn't see her either.

Enough of the pretence. I went to see how Suzanne was but she wasn't there. I looked around that end of the park.

Nothing.

Did I have a phone number? I realised I didn't have hers, or Mark's or anyone's. Curse this cloak and dagger nonsense. What could I do? Go home I suppose – there was an outside chance Mark would have taken Suzanne there... or to a hospital or to some mysterious hideout?

So I set off home, walking not running. No point in thinking about buses as that would take me as long to work out, and wait for, as to walk. I could get a taxi. Is there any point? Has Suzanne got a key? I'll get a taxi.

Chapter Six

It took me ages to find a taxi. I thought I could pick one up in the street but realised I wasn't near anywhere where taxis would wait around. After wasting time walking to where I thought I might find one I looked up the number of a local firm and telephoned. They said they would be 10 minutes – it was twenty and then they took the scenic route in heavy traffic. I would have been better walking.

When I got home I unlocked, called out and realised pretty quickly that no-one was around. I cursed myself for being pretty dumb and ineffectual.

I guess I just had to wait. But I didn't want to wait. I tried to just get on with my normal weekend stuff and started to sort some clothes for washing. But my mind was replaying events in the park. What was it about the running? It wasn't about fitness or exercise or at least not just that. It was like Suzanne was trying to recreate something, to re-enact the scene of a crime. But what crime?

The phone rang. I picked it up so quickly I must have pressed the wrong button and rejected the call. But it rang again. It was Mark. He wanted to meet. Where? At the Chocolate Factory? Are you sure? How is Suzanne? Fine, he said. Just that. No explanation. No details. Just fine. How long? Soon as you can.

So I called a taxi again. Different firm this time and a bit better response.

The Chocolate Factory is a tourist attraction on the south side of the city. As I approached I was conscious of the extent of the remodelling of our industrial history. The cottages built as hovels for workers were now preserved and presented as picture postcard posh pads from an Arts and Crafts golden age and stood out in stark contrast to the normal urban sludge. The canals, roads and railways had been altered around it.

The whole settlement was a single invention fuelled by greed and ambition but tempered by social conscience, pacifism and the abolition of slavery. It was an experiment in social engineering and a largely successful one but with an uncomfortable undercurrent from a modern perspective of Quaker puritanism. Plain dress. No alcohol. No fornication other than once or twice out of duty for the creation of the next generation of workers. But there was a bowling green, parkland with a pavilion and fishing lake, an outdoor swimming pool where doubtless the different sexes were separated through an elaborate and strictly operated timetable until it was closed down because of complaints about the noise. Fun with limits.

This was a model village in the original sense of being a model for town planning and society. A garden city now submerged by the housing estates which had grown up around it and then linked it firmly in a deathly embrace to the central city.

At the time aristocrats had a habit of moving villages. Normally because they spoiled the view of the estate from their country house. So they would simply demolish the peasants' village and rebuild it out of sight but not so far that the estate workers couldn't still walk to work at dawn. Some of these villages would be quite decoratively arranged in the picturesque manner as an expression of one-upmanship between estates.

The industrial revolution produced self-made aristocrats with a different set of social attitudes – some worse, some better. What persisted in this country, and it was by no means unique, was the architectural preference for the rural vernacular. What the British or English call a cottage is an increasingly meaningless term for a small dwelling of traditional building material. In America and Russia it means a holiday home rather than a place of work and there is still this ambiguity in what we imagine and aspire to in our dream hideaway. We imagine living in or retiring to a little cottage when the reality when most of these buildings were constructed is a simple utilitarian place to sleep between long days working in the landlord's factory.

I'd never been to this tourist attraction before but they'd done the whole Charlie and the Chocolate Factory fun experience for the kiddies. The history of chocolate, how it was made, lots of interactive games and, you've guessed it, a pile of chocolate big enough to make anyone feel sick. I wasn't looking forward to it. Mind you there was something about the smell of chocolate in the air. I remember I'd stood in for a friend on a milk round as a kid. I couldn't stand the stuff normally but when I finished that round I drank two pints of cold milk straight down without pausing for breath. It was some kind of autosuggestion. A combination of the physical activity, the smooth feel of the cold glass bottles on a hot morning (no such thing as wax or polyethylene lined cartons where I grew up) and the evocative smell of the stuff.

It was crowded. I felt awkward not having any halflings in tow. The woman who took my money to let me in looked at me strangely. "I'm meeting someone," I volunteered a bit unnecessarily. She couldn't care so I don't know why I said anything.

I wondered whether I should have some balloons or a special kind of chocolate bar in my jacket pocket so that I could be recognised. Mark hadn't been precise about where to meet and the place was a lot larger than I thought or remembered. So I just tagged along with the flow and tried very hard to learn about the history of chocolate. I was interested in the Olmec Indians and their Kakawa cocoa beans, then in the Mayas and their trade with the Aztecs. But the museum didn't seem very interested in the early history of the product. There were just a few dull looking information boards that most families walked straight by to get to the gadgets and interactive displays. The signs in the museum seemed desperate to lure you on to the industrial processes of the last couple of centuries with technical diagrams of steam engines, flashing lights and conveyer belts. But what interested me was how chocolate was used in South America for both commercial and spiritual purposes. It was the simultaneous competing worship of different guardian goddesses representing different foodstuffs that was seen as the key to enriching and balancing a well lived life.

It seemed an odd combination but maybe the commercial and religious attitudes of society had always been closely interwoven. The Spanish conquistadores who took the beans to Europe were more interested in melting down their haul of beautiful gold – destroying the cultural artworks in the process - but at least they had enough curiosity to bring home some beans. Chocolate then pretty much went under the radar and became a secret manufacturing process by monks and nuns in monasteries where rumours of its medicinal and aphrodisiac qualities thrived in its obscurity. A much more useful alchemy in the long term. It regained economic value only with the development of manufacturing processes and machinery.

When I was a kid I took part in a play at school about the invasion of Peru. Admittedly it was the Incas not the Aztecs and Peru not Mexico but I was pretty sure the Mayans and the Incas also had chocolate. It was Peter Shaffer's Royal Hunt of the Sun. The Sun in question being Atahualpa, King of the Incas and son of the Sun God. I was horrified by the violent clash of cultures and religions, by the greed and the cynical senseless slaughter. My job was to make a lot of noise about this – using whatever came to hand. The script said saws, pipes, drums and cymbals. All we had were recorders, tambourines and anything I could raid from the kitchen which I could hit with a single xylophone mallet. I had lost the xylophone and the other mallet when some idiot had thrown it out of the top window of a double decker bus when I had insisted on practicing on the way home. I also had a spoon but that was taken off me when I started hitting the heating pipes.

I simply couldn't make enough noise. I wasn't able to attract Atahualpa's attention. He seemed mesmerised by the Spanish who came riding in on what he called giant rabbits. He thought they had been sent by the gods to help with the harvest. But I could hear the Spanish soldiers, outnumbered, scared and tired. They had a priest. Their priest wanted to kill everybody. He wanted to convert them to Christianity and then burn them for being heathen. This didn't make much sense to me. I had already followed the soldiers over the mountains, night after night. I heard them talk by the fireside. I heard them plot, against the world in general and especially against their own leader. They were blinded by the Sun, blinded by gold and blinded by a religion that seemed a long way from any of our own nature and animal gods. Were our gods bloodthirsty? There were sacrifices – it's true. Some children got mummified. My uncle and cousins always used to threaten me with that although I don't think I was considered important enough to be pampered for sacrifice.

I hit that sandwich box so hard with the mallet, but Atahualpa was captured and despite filling the drama changing room with gold the bastards in 6th form killed him anyway.

When I turned to read the next information board Mark was standing closely behind me with another man I'd not seen before who grabbed me roughly by the elbow and ushered me through a door marked "Private: staff only". I allowed this to happen. Mark didn't say anything or react to my sudden exit. I was surprised that neither of them followed. The door I'd been pushed through was closed behind me. It was barely more than an ill lit cleaner's cupboard but there was room for a small desk with a low wattage angle poise lamp. As my eyes adjusted I recognised the long blond hair and small hunched figure of Suzanne. She looked up and then returned to looking through some papers.

"How are you?" I spluttered.

She looked up again and spoke softly, "Oh fine. You were useless."

"What do you mean? How the hell was I supposed to know what to do?"

"Well it was interesting and it confirmed what I suspected."

"Which is?"

"That it's pretty easy to follow the path Janet took. Scarily easy."

"Getting burnt out and having to leave her job?"

"That's a perfectly fair way of putting it. Have you heard of a runner's high?"

"No."

"What do you think it could be?"

"I don't know – some great achievement like the four minute mile?"

"Oh my God, you are a fossil from a bygone age. It's drugs or, what it comes down to really, is biochemistry. A runner's high is the release of endorphins through exercise. A bit like this place really which is what appealed to me about meeting here."

"I'd rather have the chocolate. Much less exhausting."

"But it's the same, don't you see? Endorphins work to lessen pain and decrease stress. Tryptophan, an amino acid present in small quantities in chocolate, is linked to the production of serotonin, a neurotransmitter that produces feelings of happiness. There's a bunch of other biologically active chemicals that act like a cocktail of effects on the brain. Why do you think all these middle aged women are doing aerobics. They're just a bunch of druggies seeking a natural high... or perhaps working off the effect of the chocolate!" Suzanne laughed.

This was the first time she seemed to be really relaxed and happy. Maybe it was the subconscious effect of the smell of chocolate coming under the door although if she regularly worked here I would have thought she would have built up some natural tolerance. In any case she was not making any attempt to be quiet or conspiratorial as she chatted away at normal volume.

"So what really happened to you in the park? You didn't seem to me to be experiencing a natural high."

She paused. I could have bit my tongue as her smile dropped like a stone and her facial expression changed back to anxious.

"Like I say it's a cocktail and you can get the mix wrong. Remember Janet was working on some Artificial Intelligence and Virtual Reality games. My guess is there was some kind of physical or even chemical stimulation. Something going on in the brain. When she combined that with her daily run… I don't know. I just know something went wrong. I know all her notes were handed in and she won't talk about it. Contractual confidentiality. But I did find this."

She lifted a worn leather journal tied round the middle and handed it to me. There were only a few pages in it before it stopped abruptly. I found it difficult to follow. It was written like a diary but not like any diary I had read before. No dates, no appointments… just a flurry of words leading where?

I took a deep breath and dived in. It was like a river in full flood. I was curious to see what might be downstream but knew it would be a rough and disorientating journey through unfamiliar places.

Suzanne adjusted the angle poise lamp to help me read.

Chapter Seven

Janet's Journal

The journey de jour starts from a number of different points simultaneously: Newport, Bristol, Southall, Iowa and Tibet. It all converges briefly at a small hole in the pavement dug for access to pipes on a T junction located in GU14 7PA, UK, and then instantly disperses like droplets of mercury on convex plastic.

Which droplet shall we follow?

Perhaps chance will play a hand but we will call it choice. Even on the day after an Islamic holy day where predestination might be supposed, free choice is not underestimated. In Christian terms it is driven like a nine-inch nail through the palm of destiny. In Buddhist terms it is the seemingly random but careful calculation of who should be called the reincarnation. Does the role choose the person or the person choose to follow the role allocated? Is there a meaningful difference? I don't care. I choose.

The journey starts from self-image, as if dropped naked from the sky, and will glance reflection in any shiny surface as long as the light lasts. This image is collected from other people's responses but is naturally selective and interpretive. A compliment or a criticism goes much deeper than cool analysis. But we won't dwell here. It is merely the fuel for motion, reflection and interaction.

Overall praise and security form a better springboard to increased performance than stylistic, hierarchical, socially exclusive judgement. Teach, manage, peer to peer monitoring and social horse-racing encourage and deter in equal measure. But self-analysis can be even more destructive and inaccurate. Time to move on.

So we start on a trail of aristocratic fire starters, ruined or abandoned buildings where worship and power has been a destructive moving force. Woodlands Farm with Lord Northbrook, Westbury Chapel and Manor, Hinton Ampner complete with its ghostly apparitions as we end up pursuing commerce up the Basingstoke Canal to the castle at Odiham belonging to King John at the time of his one way journey to sign the Magna Carta. All this without leaving the kitchen as we used Willy Wonka's glass elevator instead.

Fire can be the end.

Fire can be the creative levelling that makes new opportunity and construction visible. Rebuilding a canal on a river, a bat sanctuary in a disused tunnel at Greywell, a big charter of liberties for human rights from a small hunting lodge for one person. Should we plan for disaster? Perhaps. But it is hardly surprising that we don't. It is human nature to want to feel comfortable and secure. We live life as if it will last forever and it normally does until we are past caring one way or another. Sadly, if we expect to be a Phoenix, we must look for it in subtle ways – through children's children, through influence, deeds and works or in chance reflections.

Better to be reborn in a single lifetime where it is fully conscious and recognisable. So we put ourselves through the fire of nightly sleep and daily renewal. Tomorrow is another day, another chance to do it differently, do it better, to taste life with renewed vigour and appetite happy in the knowledge that if it becomes jaded and exhausted quickly then there's always mañana to look forward to. Whether it arrives is immaterial. This journey will be like that. Not so much mortification of the flesh, more a shifting landscape of time, place and physical state.

A primitive voodoo exorcised on a moment in time. A shamanistic parade of different voices. That's all it is. A schizophrenic panoply owned by an alcoholic werewolf being transformed one hair at a time.

So this is our manifesto for the free fun party. With a sickening, groaning, lurch it takes us down a plastic tube into the environs of Exeter where the fanfare of exploration sounds so far west it may well be coming from the east. Belinda mistakes Francisco for anybody. Anybody dives 132 miles to look through the bare winter trees, through the great stone gateway, over the ditch, through hedges, across the lawn, past the abandoned abbey and into the drawing room of an ex-Prime Minster of the UK. What does an ex-Prime Minister do in a drawing room? Not draw, that's for sure. They withdraw. This one was having an afternoon nap, slumped in a deep comfortable armchair by the radiator. There was a security guard somewhere but I didn't see him. There were no ghosts in cowls. No Doberman on the prowl. Just a big black car with blackened out windows poised to spew gravel from speeding wheels. Time to go before the monster wakes from beneath the trapdoor.

With all the causal awareness of a butterfly, the English tourist shelters from the storm in the basement of a four-star hotel in Mexico. The earth opens up. His marriage breaks up. He cannot send a postcard. He should have gone to the airport when the travel company begged him to. He should have left his wife before she needed counselling. The children should have gone to McDonald's. Como lo siento. The tropical palms spread-eagled on the wet rubble strewn pavement. The white pick-up truck picked up and put through the fashion shop window. It takes weeks for the storm to blow itself out across the vast oceans that separate the tourist from the ex-Prime Minister. The potted palm falls off the patio edge. The glazed pot is broken into three. Is the gentle gust a distant cousin of the spoiled brat from South America.? No. Not that you'd notice.

A reflection on the Gothic. During the past two weeks a visit to Saint Mark's Basilica in Venice. "Let us enter the church... a vast cave... vast stars, a ray or two... burning ceaselessly in the rafters." Ruskin's words resonate with the strength of the Gothic interior which is really Byzantine. A quintessential Englishness which is Italian, German and French. Sublime enthusiasm separate from Grecian proportions and mathematics. Rarely domestic. Not comfortable in Hampstead Heath. Barely comfortable in the Houses of Parliament – the accurate description of superficial bluster. The slender spires embraced by web-like embroidery. The precepts of modernism abandoned as soulless puritanism.

N'importe quoi. It is just a question of feeling. On the oche. Wicked old target. Bourré à bourrée. With pipes, you windbag. We go now to the Massif Central uplands of southern France. Far away from the North African influences of Paris we strain to hear the echoes of the Scottish Glens. Chicken or eggs? Probably neither. You might find the origin of both in the Middle Eastern desert. So perhaps North African trade is the common conduit in both Ancient and Modern times. Muslim pipes, pagan drums, gypsy dance and Gallic/Celtic aural tradition. The thin veil exposes the transparent skin to the bleached and crumbling bone. The breath whistles through our nose while we dance, drumskins taut and stretched, thumped mightily or tapped lightly with thumb and little finger whilst organs and tubes blow under the surface. Bones skittering over stones, skim on drumstick rims, sticks hitting in rhythmic swing, time to talk, time to sing, time to take the washing in, as the rain beats time on the windows again, as an Afro-Celt Sound System. Climb every mountain in every country and feel the same feeling, breathe the same thin, intoxicating air. Because it is there and there and there and here. A small figure squatted over a clay pot. There are clay sleeves baked onto his fingers. He shakes his wrists rhythmically over the belly of the pot striking alternately high and low with his hard-baked fingers. The rhythm and pitch of fashioned earth.

On the road again. Bumping over the ridges and into the potholes. We swing the jeep into the railway yard and wait. Leaves on the line. Signal delays and cable fires. Men in dark low-vis clothing trespass along the night line. Do not proceed past this point. Bogeys. Dust. Loose pins. Misaligned tracks bent in the scorching sun and freezing night temperatures. Against the odds the engine pulls into the yard. But the Punjabi exiles are dead.

Thirty degrees centigrade goes unremarked in Marathi Mumbai in Winter (the Northern European or American Winter). No sleep in the cramped upright seats during the seventeen hour connecting flights home. Pollution, noise and population pressing into capsules dispatched from home to home. Back, in my case, to the Acne Empire. The Haitch is traditionally dropped and flows down the rain filled street gutter. My companion then travels from London to Basingstoke, then via his cousin – he has so many cousins in the diaspora – to a Bengali restaurant in Four Marks. I ask him what a Bengali is doing in Mumbai and whether he is a Muslim, Hindu, Christian or Buddhist? He says it has an airport and yes. Serves me right for asking. After finishing the early shift and still jet-lagged he then takes a lift home to the English Civil War village of Cheriton from his relatives in Alton. From Alton Church to Jor-bangla temple in Bishnupur, Bankura, Bengal to Shiite Shrine in Baghdad or Buddhist temple in Bangladesh or Bhutan is only a letter away. Only one puritan, president or priest/cleric inciting tribal hatred and you're dead.

Roots, more disparate, that come unbidden from further afield. Happily dancing to the tune of a pipe around the maypole. A shawm and sackbut and hurdy gurdy and drone. Anyone could have come to Medieval England from the Middle East. So back off to Iran to remember Persia. A contemplative gong behind the steady explorations of the barbat plus a small drum, a sandy rasp echoing the melodic duet. Heading off into the dry hills in search of a courtyard garden with fountains at every corner and bright geometric patterned paths. Not yet Muslim paradise and certainly not Alexander's conquest. Something much older. Follow the sound of elongated, high singing past a twisted, starving tree and a dead sheep tethered between the rocks. A small child scampers through the dust. You are being watched. Soon they will come. But not before night has fallen. Not before you have begun to nod off in front of the dying embers of the campfire. No amount of coffee, or cold stillness of the night, will keep you awake.

Wood gauze flicker light burn moth candle wet blanket hung over straw and hazel sticks. Burnt toffee and blackened pans over a charcoal pit. Feathers flying, egg spilt, mosquitos buzz.

What was that? At first you vaguely squint and think you catch a flash of veiled white from moonlit eyes passed over by the occasional crackling fire spark. Then you hear the rustling that must have disturbed you as more of them gather. There could be thirty or forty individuals out there. Then nothing. Perhaps they have drifted through. You wait. Trying to keep quiet until you finally drop off to sleep again with an old single shot bolt action rifle resting across your lap. If they are still there then you are in no hurry to confront them. They can wait. There is no point in spilling their blood unnecessarily.

Your head drops then jerks awake. Too late. They now dance and sing in front of a revived fire. You are trussed up like a turkey while some of them go through your rucksack, provisions and spare ammunition. Then, as if it had all been a dream you enter another nightmare.

Chapter Eight

I looked up from the journal to see Suzanne staring at me intently. I shrugged my shoulders.

"What am I supposed to make of this? She's been on some sort of trip but the way it drifts around sounds like drugs to me… and she's not from Hackney or have any Indian roots I'd guess."

Suzanne didn't respond. She just put a series of airline tickets on the table. Top was a flight from Mumbai in her name. Then there was Mexico and a dozen other places.

She continued to stare at me intently.

I was missing something.

"Is this something to do with the company? Do you think she went on some business trips and just found it amusing to put some idle thoughts down?"

I was clutching at straws and Suzanne remained silent. I just wanted it to be normal because I couldn't come up with an explanation that fitted. Maybe Suzanne was right. It wasn't one thing. It was a blend of things. Long haul flights, drugs, some experimental virtual reality experience, anything else?

"Okay I'll reserve judgement and read on."

As I spoke Mark had popped his head around the door, "Not now you won't. We need to move."

"What is it – bogeys at 10 O'clock?" I found Mark's military-style instructions irritating but knew that if he said 'move' it was probably a good idea to move.

Suzanne was already up, grabbed the journal, bundled past me and was out. No-one was there to answer my question. I just had to follow.

They had gone left, back in the direction of the main entrance. No back door exit through the kitchens then. Perhaps they had received a tip off from a bit further away from someone in the street or watching a camera feed. Who knows? I had this continual duality of thought. Partly not being able to take things seriously but having to take them seriously just in case. After all I did have a brief encounter with some idiots who wanted to realign my face and I wasn't too keen on repeating that experience.

I couldn't see Mark. He was gone. But I could see Suzanne's hair jogging through the crowd and set off for it.

I kept having to stop and step around small children and their annoyed parents. I kept apologising. I virtually knocked some old lady over. Of course I stopped and helped her. I apologised again. I was really, really, really sorry but I have to go. Sorry again. I'm not sure I would make a successful secret agent. I was already beginning to attract the attention of the staff as well as a circle of visitors. But I knew where I had last seen Suzanne and it was an exit that led to a multi-storey car park. I made for that. To my surprise Mark was in a car with Suzanne already in it and it was pretty much behind the exit to the first car park. I was expecting I would have lost them, have to walk the streets and then call a taxi again. I jumped in and we were off. Well, we had to wait for the barrier. This is reality after all.

We made for the motorway signs out of the city but we were still in a residential area. It was slow progress. Buses, pedestrian crossings, roadworks. Mark was fast and slightly illegal in terms of speed but not reckless. He kept looking in his rear-view mirror. There was a black van he noticed but it turned off. Suddenly it re-emerged from a side road and hit the rear of our car spinning the back end sideways. I was in the back seat with Suzanne and we took the full whiplash effect. I must have sworn or said something. Nobody else spoke. Mark just revved the accelerator to a high-pitched whine but we didn't seem to be going anywhere until the rear tyres re-engaged, screeched and we were off with an acrid smell of exhaust smoke. He mounted the pavement and managed to get in front of the next vehicle then took a left with some uncomfortable speed bumps, swerving around those annoying width restrictions with bollards.

I looked back and wished I hadn't. No black van but the jarred muscles in my neck made me swear at the top of my voice again.

"Be quiet," said Suzanne, "it's not helping Mark."

"It's a cul de sac, damn it," she added immediately, breaking her own rule as we headed towards a brick wall.

"No it's not," said Mark, "they wouldn't have all this traffic calming nonsense if there wasn't a useful cut through to somewhere."

Sure enough when we got closer to the wall we could see there was a gap to the left by some garages where you could access another road. Mark had to mount a raised area with brick paviours and drop down back onto tarmac and then there was an exit onto a major road.

Traffic was heavy. I looked behind again. It hurt but I just grunted. I couldn't see anything but thought I could hear the whine of an over-revved engine even with the windows closed. Perhaps the re-arrangement of the back end of the car and created a gap in the chassis as our engine, even idling at this junction, sounded louder than it had before.

I didn't understand why Mark hadn't exited onto the road straight away but he was waiting for a gap to turn right and when he went he certainly went pretty quickly. I kind of admired the fact that he was still obeying basic traffic rules. Maybe he was just using common sense as there was no point getting side swiped again.

Unfortunately it also meant that the black van had time to see us exit and, eventually, despite the narrow traffic calming obstacles, follow. Mark didn't see it in the mirror, he was too busy looking for a gap in the traffic, but I did. I decided not to say anything. Not out of petulance because I'd been told to shut up. Okay a little bit from that but I also didn't see what difference it would make or improve the situation in any way.

We were starting to get further out of the city. The shops and houses were not crowding the road anymore. There were occasional trees, open spaces, allotments. The traffic started to thin and we started to go faster. Faster and faster until the trees started to blur like the hedgerow from a train.

For some reason I imagined what it would be like to be a chicken or a young calf in the back of lorry being taken for slaughter. I was banging around in a confined space. Banging against metal and my fellow travellers. I could hardly keep my feet and would have fallen if there was anywhere to fall.

I decided I was a calf. I knew this because I could remember the farm. If I'd been a chicken I would just have a memory of being pecked at in a cage. I couldn't remember too much about the farm but I remembered the sensation of light, occasional grass fields with hedgerows and trees, occasionally a big open barn with slippery concrete floors and ramps covered in straw and cow dung. This was a combination of the two, hard floor and rushing light, but much more difficult because of the sickening whirlwind motion of the entire world around me.

Eventually we started to slow down almost to stop then there was an uneven potholed road and we came to a thundering stop. Although I wanted the journey to end I could smell something much worse in my nostrils here that made me wish we had kept going. It was the smell of fear, the smell of death. The other animals started to panic. There was a lot of noise. Clanking metal hooks and chains on rails, conveyor belts, saws, knives, power tools, slicing, stabbing, sluicing.

We were on a rough track in a yard somewhere well off the main roads. It was countryside, trees and hedgerows but with a big warehouse behind us, barbed wire and spiked security fences all around. There were a few trucks at the far corner by the warehouse. Meat wagons, farm produce... it was a slaughterhouse.

Damn me. The black van had rammed us again. I woke from my reverie as three men dressed in black piled out of the van and started pulling at the doors and tried to smash the windows. Mark had set the child lock and the back doors weren't budging.

Although our doors were locked Mark was already out of the car and whacked the first assailant with what looked like a retractable police stick. He caught him full on the front of the head and he went straight down. He then managed to get a side swipe at the other attacker on that side of the car but only managed to strike him on his raised arm as he swerved his torso and head away from the blow. This guy had some sort of shorter cosh with which he had been trying to break the window. He switched hands with this now into his left and squared up to Mark.

Suzanne was jumping about in the back seat like a jack in a box. When she realised she wasn't going to make any headway with the door she started climbing over me and into the front seat. It was pretty tight and she had to keep twisting her torso and fall head first into the front well.

The first attacker started to groan and come to. This distracted the second and Mark made another lunge, this time taking the guy's left leg at the knee. There was a horrible cracking sound. I don't know whether it was broken but he fell over his colleague and Mark followed up with a couple of blows to the head and a kick for good measure.

By this time Suzanne had unlocked the doors and pushed her way out. The third attacker was watching what was going on at the other side of the car but had already turned to run back to the van as Suzanne rugby tackled him from behind and sit on him face down.

As the danger seemed to have past I thought this would be a good time to get out and get involved. Mark was just standing over his charges, bent slightly forward and breathing heavily. So I tried to restrain the third attacker who was turning and now wrestling with Suzanne. I held one of his arms while Suzanne sat on the other and hit him repeatedly in the face with both fists.

"Alright, alright," he pleaded, "you win. We'll go back to Level Zero."

It was only then that I recognised him. He was from my workplace, but he wasn't a security guard. The last time I had seen him was when

I was trying to get another mug from the kitchen cupboard and he was in there, suit and tie, getting in the way and reheating some vegan stew in the microwave. As I tried to dance around him in the narrow workplace kitchen, we exchanged pleasantries about the weather and how many people were expected to share such a small space. I don't think he worked on my floor because I didn't see him again. Maybe he didn't even normally work on that site. Who knows? I just know he wasn't security staff – my guess would be a junior admin role, perhaps finance data entry. Something repetitive and not too demanding where quantity rather than quality was key.

"I know you, don't I?" I enquired.

"I don't think so."

"I've seen you in the kitchen at work."

"I don't work in a kitchen."

"This is useless," I said turning to Suzanne, "what are we going to do with them?"

"We're not taking them with us if that's what you think," said Suzanne.

That made him nervous.

"We should have used the gun," he said.

"What?"

"Yeah, one of the guards had a gun. It's in the glove compartment. But he said it would use up too many points and we could take you without it."

I could see he regretted straightaway telling us this as if it was something he was told not to mention and so couldn't help blurting it out because it was so much on his mind. But it wasn't mention of the gun that was troubling me.

"What do you mean points?"

"You know. You need credit to buy ammunition and it takes 50 points away every time you use it."

Suzanne looked at me and there was a mutual recognition in making the obvious deduction. "You… think… this… is… some… sort… of… game…" she spluttered. With every word she started hitting him again and again.

I let go of his arm and stood up. I don't think he was badly hurt. Suzanne wasn't using her full force. She was slapping him more in frustration than attack. But I could see he was stunned, bruised and bleeding from the side of his lip and one nostril.

I looked round and Mark had his head buried in the car. He was fetching out a few personal items, the journal, a bottle of water, car documents.

"This car's shot," he said, although he didn't mean it literally, "we'll take the van."

"What about this lot?" I asked.

"Leave them."

"Shouldn't we call the police?" I asked.

"Yes if you want," he replied, "but I'm not hanging about to make a statement."

"I'm not sure that's a good idea, just leaving them here."

We both looked at Suzanne for the casting vote. "Mark's right. We can't stay here in case there are more of them and we can't take them with us. Why would we want to? They would be more trouble than they're worth. We need to get away first and then talk about it."

I was uncomfortable with this. Despite not having a great experience last time that I tried to report violence to the correct authorities. I was treated like I was involved in some sort of gang warfare where I was equally guilty and just trying to make trouble for someone that I had a grudge against. But my family upbringing had instilled a fundamental belief that law enforcement was a good thing and I felt I was getting dragged by Mark and Suzanne into something where my actions would be increasingly questionable.

But they were already in the front seat of the van and ready to go. Two of the men were now getting to their feet and I didn't want to be left alone with them.

I realised we had been quite lucky. Mark had taken them by surprise. We might not be that lucky a second time.

I climbed into the cab. "Budge up." It was one of those cabs where you could fit three across the front seat. Mark was swinging the van around while I was trying to find the seatbelts.

"You were pretty useless back there," Suzanne said to me.

"So you think I'm a trained assassin in my spare time? Truth was I must have dropped off, with the motion of the car, because I was having the weirdest dream. I must have heard some animals because I was imagining being taken to slaughter."

"The knacker's yard was shut. Quiet as the grave. That's why we tried to hide out there. Did you actually dream you were an animal?"

"Yes."

"Well maybe you could be more use carrying on with the journal then. Janet imagined she was an animal at one point but like everything in her narrative it seemed to shift in and out of focus."

Chapter Nine

Janet's Journal

You are a baby caribou. One of several million crossing the Canadian tundra in Spring. Two white wolves (there must be more hidden from view) are following the pack. They run straight into the edge of the herd to cause panic. Why do we always do what they want? We panic. Is it because our parents fear for the young? Or is it because if we run we won't expect it to happen to us? Safety in the herd. Most will survive. It will happen to another – to that old one that can't keep up. She's had a good innings, can't give birth, she's had her time. But the herd splits straight down the middle. Someone should have said which way to run. As long as you stay in the centre you are safe. Even now if we keep running we can be safe, we can easily stay ahead. The wolves are just strolling around making occasional little runs, saving their energy. The wolf has no stamina. Surely they will give up after a mile or two.

But the herd splitting enables the wolves to target individuals. Individual calves that is. Where is my mother? I've lost my mother? I can't see her. Can't smell her. Even now I am safe as long as I don't stumble. I stumble. The wolf, exhausted, tries to catch it's breath before the others arrive. Then, casually, it takes it's first bite from the living calf.

For the others the migration continues. We always expect that we will be amongst them.

Ivor! Billy! Come in for tea! What is it? Gruts again. Three years of gruts and then we will taste grass, trees and leaves. Let's imagine for now that it is now, now that it's not gruts for tea again, and move on.

Indecision, pleasure, exercise, resolution (again), uncertainty, being in several places. Transience gives the past flavour and the future appetite. But which identity to pursue, which passport to which destination? I know where I am going but not how to get there. It should be intrinsically linked, previously liked and linear progression from appetite to satisfaction but it is the pauses, the gaps, the aftertaste and reflection which holds the rush, the flood, the anticipation of whatever it is we smell and smile.

The vagaries of chance and time roll. The weighted dice wobbles and settles on the Free State of Bavaria. Organ music is playing somewhere beyond the slit castle window high up on the north wall above the tallest of the Austrian Pines. Is it loud enough to cover the sound of the grappling hook scuffing down the wall and lodging in the interstices between the corner of the window and the stone ledge? Who cares? There is no other choice. Does the lady really love Cadbury's milk chocolate? Or is the night intruder awaiting your entry? Only one way to find out. Take off your skis, throw the rope and climb. In snow-born sorrow and exhaustion you slump over the parapet. Too weak to do anything other than accept your fate. Thankfully the masked phantom Michael Crawford is nowhere to be seen. Neither is the milk-white mädchen. Instead the broad grin of a naked black friend who offers a hot drink and the chance to slump on the red velvet cloth.

Off into the Black Forest of tall pines packed densely together for mile after mile. Up to where Germany meets France and Switzerland. Vast, untamed, un-regenerated, unexploited forest – at least in the Teutonic psyche, where it obliterates the rich and tropical jungle of other's imaginings. A place of safety from the hot Mediterranean sunlight and the healthy, outgoing, friendly family tendencies of well-adjusted citizens. A range of angular, hidden slopes and slides, peaks and dives. The falcon swoops and stuns the slow-moving pigeon step by step, half-dazed, treading the air in an explosion of feathers. When the peregrine swoops and falls silently as a tree in a forest there is no butterfly born on the opposite side of the world. This is a place where dark resentment, jealousy, suspicion and paranoid psychosis can stalk like a grey wolf snarling at a basket of new-born puppies. So we head for any clearings. We want to see the short-mown grazing of the islands of sunlight, made all the more intense by the dark shadows surrounding it.

We are an island race. Everyone is. A continent is connected to itself and not immune from insularity. An island is the first to notice a change in the sea but a continent is only an island with more self-esteem. An island race has more incentive to trade and travel and think of itself in relation to others. The island traveller truly understands space and the stars that give it shape. A map of our Treasured Island falls into the wrong hands. One foot and a parrot included. The power and psychology of a territorial map leads us to believe there is a singular shortest path to treasure. It also implies that it lies in a foreign land and that we have to violate a border of unknown difficulty and danger to get there. The grass being greener on someone else's island. This is the curse of the island race. Being able to see the shore, someone else's shore. You can't see that in the forest. The feeling of being unable to get to that shore, and/or the disappointment of getting to that shore and finding our neighbour's island doesn't match the island of our dreams, is not a problem. Is it better to dream and never journey or to let travel broaden the mind with real and psychological movement? Let us do both.

Tracking Bactrian camels over the Gobi Desert from Northern China to Southern Mongolia. They can see you at 5 kilometres and run for 70. Patience and persistence. Without these qualities, luck is impossible. Without these, determination and optimism cannot thrive. The desert survives by contradicting everything we know from other places. In the desert the camel must drink snow.

The Aztecs built their temples in the West so that Toltecs couldn't get up the steps past the CCTV with their tanks. Fourteen foot ditches on the sides of the road. Sensors in the sewers. The computations within the temple walls bore astronomical significance to the Sun Alliance. Now a Cap has been put on the pinnacle. One of two non-identical Gemini twins. One in the West and one in the East. Two hearts beat as one before the sacrifice of network-centric ignorance.

It doesn't matter whether you start in the West and travel East or vice versa. You end up in the same place. So let's start in the South West. The water and the pupils engulf the hockey field after the school washroom taps and the stormy weather are both left on. The Valency Valley has matured and deepened. Butterscotch rocks sucked and spat out at Werther's Grandfather. The Birch at Lamorna Cove paints rocks above the rockless beach. Posed for the camera in green and red as the saw rocks back and forth on the wooden block resting on the trestle table. Four-wheeled carts stacked impossibly high with hay sausage rolls along the narrow deep cut lanes. The smell of crushed apples ferments in the nostrils as the thunder sets up the seagulls like a rocket in the night. Pots and pans knock against each other suspended on lines in the wind. I sneeze and snore. Charles Richter measures it and several bridges collapse.

Stepping stones are now the only way to cross the broad, shallow, but fast moving river. But even some of these have been washed away giving the river a gap-toothed dingle-dangler's grin. By a series of death-defying leaps with full packs (with no run up) we land on the inadequate landing strip with suddenly arrested momentum. We slide and fall like a Jumbo Jet trying to land on an aircraft carrier. But the river isn't that deep. You would have had to be very determined to make a fist of drowning. It's more a question of pride versus humiliation. The mockery of misjudging, slipping and ending up bashing your head or shin on a sharp rock and lying belly up in the freezing water. The rites of passage paid to the river gods in waterproof skin. The ferryman is laughing all the way to the bank. The wicker man rocks and creaks with laughter and the ivy lady giggles while her hair dangles and dances from the trees.

Then we all piled into the Land Rover which was winched up over the riverbank into the wooded foothills of Kingley Vale in West Sussex in the South East. We took the steepest track and headed straight for the ruined flat barn overlooking Chichester harbour. In the narrow portcullis window was placed an envelope with our next destination.

We weren't sure whether this was a treasure hunt, an elaborate hoax or a trap. We half-expected the destination to be the parliament building in Kathmandu, Nepal. It was the suicide door in Norwich Cathedral. We were asked to climb, beyond where the public are normally allowed to go, to give a rendition, as best we could, of How Much is that Doggie in the Window on piano accordion and Baritone Sax; then drop anti-animal testing literature on the assembled congregation. Strange that we hadn't been asked to wear superhero (U.S. Trademark) costumes but then our animal lib group never did have any sense of style. I thought the Baritone Sax said style, so we agreed to do it during some suitably bland, but appropriate, reading or hymn like All Things Bright and Beautiful, All Creatures Great and Small.

Up. When the door swings open, we walk out into the suicide opening. Someone must have made a noise or there was some pre-arranged signal from the nave because we saw faces turn towards us. With arms outspread we hush the gathered throng. The cameraman from BBC Look East refocuses. Oblivious to the innocent, we give a lusty, if flawed, rendition of our little ditty but the end comes sooner than expected. I dropped the saxophone. It nearly totalled the verger. So without dropping our leaflets (which had been the inadvertent cause of finding out the sax wasn't properly connected to the neck strap) we beat a hasty retreat down the stairs and out of the transept door with mumbled apologies to ourselves and anyone else that would listen. We left the mangled corpse of the saxophone with Edith Cavell.

It took no more than four or so minutes to pack our meagre belongings, strap what footwear and clothing, food and 'useful things' we had and trudge off in roughly the right direction. We tried to keep to the main road, which arced in a south-westerly direction, thus prescribing our actual destination, but it felt good to be on the road again. Down to Thetford. Past the pines of Dad's Army. Then hitchhiking through Chelsea and along the Hog's Back. Dropped in the vicinity of the Hotel overlooking the demolished Gas Tower of Aldershot. Of the Lords and Ladies who entered the selection only 11 were chosen to ride in the Aphex Twin's Daimler Ferret Mark 3. We revisited the food science of Mars but decided it was too dangerous.

As soon as we reached the outskirts of town a torrential downpour started. Then the wind picked up and debris flew in swirling eddies. Then the wind suddenly decided on a direction and everything went south. We kept close to the walls looking for somewhere to shelter. The rain felt like it was trying to drive horizontally, stinging your face if you were unwise enough to try and look where you were going.

Eventually, when the storm was getting too much for us, we saw a half-opened garage door in a row of other garages behind some shops. The shops themselves were closed. Some were boarded up. Others had metal grilles or shutters. One of us bent down to look under the garage door. Although it was dark inside, and the whole world was gloomy and glowering, someone said it was empty. So we all piled in. It wasn't empty. Lined up on the far wall were...six people dressed as Bunny Girls. Three of them were men. Apparently they were on their way to the Rocky Horror Picture Show at the Alexandra Palace and had taken shelter on the way. Behind us entered three Gothic vampire punks. I felt distinctly like my namesake in the film but they were a friendly bunch. Most of them smoked and, after a while, raining or not, we preferred to be on our way to fill our lungs with air or water – both felt healthy and connected to the life of the Earth. Strange that the planet should be named after one of the less dominant characteristics. Coming from Space you would be more likely to call it Air or Water.

The sea in the air gradually withdrew and the air, which had been thumping like a sub-woofer in a converted hot hatchback, faded to a dripping trickle. The world appeared metal grey-green after the storm. It brooded, but it no longer threatened. All passion spent. In fact it was overdrawn, in debt and sagged loosely and wetly on the pavements and in the grass. Most of the people seemed to have been washed away. From the corner of the flyover by the ring road you could see the clock tower of the library down in the town. There was no point now in trying to return those library books. You could also see the floodwaters lapping around the top of the pediment supporting it. What looked like the tops of cars, furniture at jaunty angles and was that a coffin floating by it's top window? The water was brown and dirty, almost black. The dirt was from people and things now sanitised and washed clean. A river of sorrow from which you should not drink.

Don't swallow the passing of time. In the darkness you will see the faces of lost generations. I supposed we should have looked for people to help, rescued Grannies and their cats from rooftops but, like some law enforcement officers totally swamped in New Orleans, we decided that absence would make the heart grow fonder. We turned and ran for higher ground.

The blue delta opens out before the levy. The juke joints reached by boat in a flooded downtown suburb. A black dog swims from pier to boat. A box floats by. Close to the source there is a strange sensation when the levee breaks. It keeps on raining. There is no place to stay. Crying won't help you. Shouting won't help you. Praying won't do any good. The Bible belt tightened, the lightening frightened, the logic loosened and the odds shortened. Call the National Guard to guard the nation from the people, for the people, by the people, shoot the looters, fry the perps, hang the weathermen, climate change storm bringers for Armageddon Southern-style.

One sound among many stayed with me. The sound of plastic and metal bins slapping against walls as the water flowed along the currents and counter-currents, backwashes and eddies. Loose black refuse sacks would slap against buildings, doors and windows; remain there for a few seconds and then peel off and fall back into the water. Sometimes the bag would be shredded and the waste washed along, spread out or sunk together with objects of a life no longer wanted or needed. The dolls and toy soldiers, the food cartons, the intimate objects of love and death, the letters, the consumer packaging, the broken and the useless, the detritus of necessity and greed. As the day wore on a clean core of swinging moonglow remained.

The waters stayed for what seemed like weeks. Weeks in which the colour became mid-brown and stagnant. The air hummed with helicopter swarms of fresh flies. As the water began to recede on a daily basis a succession of tidelines were stratified on the sides of buildings. It marked the passage of time but also emphasised the static viewpoint we held on the high ground with a few companions. But the time had come when it was not only safe to move on but necessary. We were fortunate to have been well fed and had plenty of bottled water but we could see on the faces of our hosts, and from the conversations not meant for our ears, that the generous supplies were also receding. Plus we itched with impatience. The temptation to move too soon was very strong. I guess we were waiting for a sign. Not a kingfisher but a dove with an olive branch. The waters had to make peace with the earth. Unfortunately we didn't have the luxury of a wooden cruise ship but at least we didn't have the annoyance of pairs of animals trying to eat each other. There were scavengers though, amongst the bloated corpses of animals and men. No crocodiles or alligators but plenty of crows and a few monstrous eels, at least we guessed that was what was making the water slither and ripple.

When the time came the mud dried and cracked. The world was dirty but able to breathe again. We set off in the direction of the mid-day Sun to the next range of hills. These used to be sandstone. A good deal of this had been washed away and levelled. Where the sandstone was hard enough (and mixed with enough iron) it protruded in new fantastic head and face-like shapes like malignant cobras.

We didn't see many other survivors, which surprised us, but there was plenty of evidence of their existence. Property had been broken into, windows smashed, goods piled up in gardens and then left as it dawned on people that it probably wasn't worth taking a 75" High Definition LED TV when there was no electricity. The value of electrical goods was outstripped by the humble cabbage. Nonetheless the instinct to hoard useless objects in anticipation of better times was obviously still strong.

Those who had less to lose fared better. They adopted a positive attitude and made the best of new opportunities. I guess thieves and crooks are natural optimists and should be praised for their lack of hypocrisy compared to, say, captains of industry. They are honest about one thing: their fundamental selfishness. They are the natural embodiment of the will to survive. Not the noblest pursuit but common dry ground we begrudgingly share.

I saw a badly handwritten notice on a wonky telegraph pole offering to clear fallen trees and debris with petrol driven chainsaws. What made me chuckle was that the rates they were quoting were higher than the national debt of a third world country. It just cheered me up. That people would want to tidy up, rebuild and exploit each other again. After all you wouldn't want to argue rates after the job with a hot, sweaty, tired and emotional guy with a chainsaw.

So it's going to be like the Wild West again is it? Hell no. Even in a lawless society what is most striking was how far some people would go to help each other. The first people I saw were carrying a few young and old piggy-back style to higher ground. The people helping, and the people being helped, probably weren't close relatives judging by the mix of clothing styles and skin tones. They were just people. People helping people.

We greeted them, and wished them well, but we needed or wanted to move fast and so we couldn't, or wouldn't, help. I'm not sure there's a difference. We did give them some water and a little food. Once we made the high ground of the ridgeway we turned east towards London. From this vantage point we could see more of the extent of the devastation. Once a busy road, this route was now empty except for the occasional slumped figure in the ditch that we didn't want to poke to see whether it was alive or dead. Alive would be worse.

As we approached the other end of the ridge before the land began to fall from the Hogs Back towards Guildford we saw four hooded figures standing by a tree. As we approached, and they must have been able to see us for half a mile, they began to shift their weight from one foot to the other as if uncomfortable with the wait. They all had their hands thrust deep in their pockets, save one who brandished a long fork in each hand. We moved on. Their heads and eyes swivelled to follow but they didn't attempt to follow with the rest of their bodies though we kept looking back as if inviting them to chase.

Chapter Ten

Wherever we were going we seemed to have arrived. I'd imagined some big safe house in the country with a barn to hide the van but we seemed to be on a suburban street somewhere and we had just parked off the road in front of a semi-detached house with a few straggly roses in a bed by a dwarf wall. The rest was red tarmac edged with pale concrete crazy paving.

"How far have you got?" Suzanne asked me.

"Somewhere near Guildford."

"Good, almost there then."

I wasn't quite sure what she meant by that. I was pretty sure we were still in the West Midlands.

"I'll tell you something, Suzanne, I don't think this is a game. Whatever crazed experience Janet has been through, or imagines she's been through, it's not based on a console game. With those security guys it was all shoot 'em up and score points. This journal's not like that. You could say that there are mentions of different scenario options and dangers and quests associated with exploring different levels of a game, or at least locations, but it's not mechanical in the way I would expect. There's no maths indicative of losing or gaining life points or scoring criteria to achieve some mission or objective as you would expect. It's more like a diary of different thoughts in different locations. Okay it's a crazy fucked up psychedelic life but in the way she stumbles from one crisis to another, with an occasional pause to reflect on the meaning of it all, then it isn't so different from anybody else's life. It certainly resonates with what my life has been like in the last few weeks."

Suzanne looked at me reflectively as if about to agree then just ignored me and pushed past me into the house where Mark had just juggled a set of keys and entered.

I followed.

"So what's this place?" I asked.

"Hugh's Mum's," Mark answered.

"So where's Hugh's Mum?" I asked.

"Dead."

That was the end of that conversation.

We scouted around. We chose bedrooms although none of us had anything with us like luggage or even a coat that we could mark out our territory with. The place was still furnished as if someone had just stepped out. There were ornaments on the shelf and photographs on the wall including one of Hugh's graduation and one I guessed must have been him as a child with another boy – a brother?

But there was nothing in the fridge to eat. There were some old teabags and a kettle. That would have to do. The coffee was unusable. It had gone black and stuck to the bottom of the jar. There was no milk.

We relaxed with our tasteless hot drinks. I hadn't realised quite how tired I was. Suzanne, and particularly Mark, must have felt the same. They weren't very talkative.

Eventually, when I couldn't stand the silence any longer, and I thought at least Mark was about to fall asleep, I did my annoying kid act and asked the parents in a loud and whiny voice, "What are we going to do now then?"

More silence.

Mark looked at me. So he was awake.

"I'm going to dump the van and bring back some food. Then we'll sleep. We can talk in the morning."

"That sounds a bit like we'll talk later...again," I said.

Suzanne could see that Mark was about to get angry, possibly violent, and intervened, "I'll dump the van...I have an idea for it. You both get some sleep and I'll wake you when there's some food to eat."

"We don't need to do anything elaborate with the van," said Mark. "I'm not interested in torching it to mask fingerprints or anything like that. Taking the van is the least of our worries."

"I wasn't going to drive it off a cliff or anything. I just know a place to park it where it won't arouse any interest for at least a few weeks or maybe never. I expect it will rust and the tyres go flat."

"They might have some GPS tracker on it," Mark added.

"So? The place I'm thinking about is not that close to here that they would find us. There is public transport that connects but you could go in any direction. I reckon I can be back in an hour."

Mark held his hand to his head. "What I mean is that they will already have a breadcrumb trail to this house if they have been tracking the van. I didn't think about it before. I wasn't thinking."

"I have some skills," I said.

I think that statement surprised me more than it did them.

"I have access to the vehicle tracking system at work," I said. "I can't delete the record because that would be impossible and would also highlight the anomaly on all the weekly reports. But I can just mark it as private and non-work related. It won't show up on any of the normal information and, if I can remember it, I think there's a way to subtly change one of the destination co-ordinates without it showing up on the audit trail. One of the transport guys was having an affair once and we discovered a loophole where his married lady friend was using system access to make a stop at a private residence look like a half hour break at a local transport cafe. She moved on and I don't think they ever tightened up on the system access or disciplined her although they did sack the driver later for some completely unrelated vehicle safety issue."

"Can you do it from here?" Suzanne asked.

"I just need an internet device. A laptop or something with a keyboard would be really nice but a phone would do."

"Does it make sense to use someone else's phone, to mask who made the changes?"

"I'll be using my username and password so it doesn't really matter. It'll be traceable if someone knows where to look. You can always discover stuff. I thought the point was just to make it more difficult. Buy us some time."

Then I thought about it. I thought about why they chose to get me involved in all this. I thought about why they were not surprised or amazed I had access to the company's computer systems.

"You do realise you are probably going to get me put in jail?"

"I don't think so," said Mark.

"When all this is done …and I hope it will be some day…I was kind of hoping to go back to work."

"I can't promise that," said Mark, "but I don't think you'll end up in jail."

He didn't say any more. I waited, but neither of them said any more.

I sighed.

They were waiting for me to volunteer. I normally make it a rule not to volunteer for anything stupid or dangerous but there didn't seem any other options being offered.

"Okay Suzanne, get rid of the van. I'll give you an hour and then I'll start to log in. Assuming I can pass the multi-factor authentication, and assuming I haven't already been blocked as a hacker by external firewalls, and assuming I haven't already been flagged up as a dangerous ex-employee with a grudge by internal security, then it'll take me about 10 to 20 minutes or so to cover your tracks. Any chance of another cooked breakfast when you get back?"

"I'll see what I can do – although it might be the middle of the night when you get it. The nearest store is quite a walk away."

Suzanne then turned and left through the kitchen door, leaving me with grumpy Mark. Maybe she thought we needed some male bonding time. Or maybe she just felt the need to be doing something so volunteered to get rid of the van.

"So, never mind Janet, tell me about Mark?"

"I'm going to bed, that's all you need to know about Mark."

"You used to work at Harman, didn't you? Is that how you got to know Janet?"

"I always liked Janet. You know you get an instant feeling about people. Is it pheromones or something?"

"You mean you liked her because she smelled nice? That's called perfume."

"You know when you instantly like or dislike someone? Maybe it's their body language, or a way of expressing something, their sense of humour or maybe it is their natural body odour; I don't know. In my line of work I guess you become more sensitive to observing and taking note of the little things people do that tell you more about them. Under the perfume. Under the clothes. Under the pretence. At a basic animal level."

"So are you a doctor or an anthropologist?"

"Definitely not a doctor. Is there an equivalent to the Hippocratic oath for hurting people? If so I made that one."

"So you go round observing and hurting people?"

"You know what I do, or what I did. Some of it anyway. Yes I worked at Harman, before that I was in the police. Before that I was in the Army... briefly."

"You don't look old enough to be an army veteran or retiree from the police."

"It's the mileage and the damage not the age. You don't have to be old to be an army veteran and I didn't retire from the police. I just, kind of, went on secondment."

"You mean undercover?"

"That carries a whole baggage with it that it is a long way from the truth. It would be more accurate to say I'm on a gap year."

"I don't know much about the police but I don't think they do gap years. Did they find out about your cross dressing and want to give you some time to sort out your gender alignment?"

"I'm not being paid so that's how I look at it. And no, my appearance at the cinema was a bit of a one off. Phe made me up as a bit of a joke. I enjoyed it though. I might do it again. Changing clothes is not the same as changing gender as you well know. Now I really am going to bed."

Mark got up from the kitchen table, groaned at the effort and made his way to the door. As he was going through it he turned and asked, "You do recognise me from Harman, don't you?"

"Vaguely. You were on the front desk doing security, sometimes, but I didn't really take any notice."

"Yes, I know."

Mark went up the stairs and sounded like he was trying to clean his teeth in the bathroom using his finger as a brush. I sat for a while just trying to process what Mark said. It would make sense of why he wasn't bothered about telling anything to the police. He was probably reporting it anyway. But it didn't make sense to me. Either he was in the police or he wasn't. I got the impression that he wasn't.

I should have quizzed him on the circumstances of how and why he left the army. I guess he could have been invalided out with some non-visible injury. But then again he could have taken a swipe at some five star Colonel, or be caught selling weapons to terrorists, or spent time in the glasshouse for not having polished his brass belt buckle so that you could see your face in it. I'm not sure that any of that would have best qualified him for a career in the police but then again it helps to be able to think like a criminal to successfully track and catch criminals so maybe he had picked up some skill or experience they found useful. I always thought being in the police or being the local hooligan were two sides of a very thin coin. The only difference being that a local hooligan was a stress free and viable career that would be properly appreciated by colleagues and friends.

I still wasn't tired so I picked up the journal again as I wondered absentmindedly what Suzanne was doing.

Sue (as she preferred to think of herself but nobody ever called her that) was driving around in circles trying to find the place she'd thought of to hide the van. It was getting dark and she had only been to this place a couple of times, and on foot, so quite reasonably she asked herself why would she have taken note any of the one-way roads and those that end in traffic blocking bollards? Besides, she thought, I'm not sure I trust that idiot John to hack the system. It won't hurt to drive around in a slightly random way before I get there.

She also wanted some time to herself. Away from the boys and their tiresome alpha male nonsense. She hadn't asked Mark and Hugh (or John) to get involved. Mark had been sweet on Janet. Not as much as I loved Janet, she thought. But Mark clearly cared about her. Not like a father or brother, more like an uncle. He didn't want to see her come to any harm and was prepared to step in and do whatever was needed for the sake of 'the family'.

As she drove on into the dark neon-lit streets her mind was fully on the others, starting with Mark and Hugh.

When Mark first introduced Hugh I thought they were lovers but I never saw them show any signs of physical intimacy. No holding hands, no tell-tale looks of understanding between their eyes and certainly no kissing. Mind you, with Hugh's pipe I can't say I would blame Mark for keeping his distance. He said he was a friend of Mark's. He looked like some sort of science boffin but never said much to me. Both of them were basically just listening. But whenever I mentioned Janet's work and the experimentation on virtual reality, or implied that there might be some sort of drug stimulant involved, then he got very interested and animated. He would quiz me on Janet's behaviour, how she felt, what she ate and drank, whether her pupils were dilated and obscure physical details like that. That pretty much told me all I needed to know. Mark must have brought Hugh in as some sort of specialist analyst, perhaps a qualified doctor.

So what about the gorgeous and huge Pheona? Pheona had introduced herself as a singer in an Irish folk group I'd vaguely heard of called Drogheda. I asked her if that was where she had come from as I knew about the town on the border of County Louth. She laughed and said she was born in London then explained that it meant 'bridge' or 'bridge of the ford' as the group felt that their music was a bridge between this world and the world of Celtic myth and fantasy. I'd never heard her sing but one time when I arrived she was playing a plain old battered tin whistle and it was beautiful. I told her that her playing was mesmerising, like the pied piper. She said that was because she was the patron saint of drunkards, poets and stargazers. She implied that she had known Janet before I had. In her typical rambling way of talking she said she had met Janet one night many years ago as a curious hunter. She said she was one of the three sisters of Orion who had banded together to fight the goddess of the hunt, the bull and the scorpion. I presumed this was some reference to the stars, horoscopes, tarot or astrology and I've always had nothing but contempt for that nonsense so I didn't ask her anything further. Little did I know at the time that I was supposed to be the other sister in her little fantasy world.

After going around the one way system three times (perhaps they should call it the three way system) I found the slip road to the dead end I was looking for, below the towering viaduct and railway bridge. There were a few lock ups and the odd wino and tramp with fearsome dogs but I knew a piece of wasteland to one side that was tucked between two walls. From the front you could just see a cavern of buddleia and bramble. I got out of the van to double check that no-one was sleeping in there and that there were no hidden objects like lumps of concrete that might stop the van getting in through the vegetation. There was a shopping trolley, plastic bags and some sodden rags. I moved the trolley and tentatively poked the rags with a stick just to make sure they didn't hide a person or animal. There was nothing there so I carefully reversed the van in. The buddleia snapped and broke but the bramble just reclosed over the gap beautifully. In fact I struggled to get the door open and squeeze out again. On the driver side I had left it a little bit too tight against the wall. But I was slim and although my hair certainly looked like I was dragged through a hedge backwards I managed to get out. I took a small branch from the buddleia which had broken off and used it to tease the bramble to cover up some final touches and got a few additional cuts and scratches on my bare forearms. Probably should have dressed differently for this (and put my hair back).

I looked around and listened. I couldn't hear or see anyone but frankly I didn't care if I had been seen. All the better if someone broke into the van and used it as a drug den or a pop-up brothel.

As I moved away I did see a group of three tramps slumped against a wall a few hundred yards up the road and I had to walk past them which was a bit scary. I had kept the broken stick and they didn't challenge me or ask me for anything. If they had seen the van or associated me with it then they probably thought it best not to see or hear anything. They would observe the code of the down and out street monkeys and not see, hear or speak any evil unless or until there was some profit in it.

It was a long walk to the all-night supermarket and there were a few other encounters along the way before I felt confident to throw away the stick. I had a mission and I wasn't going to let anything stop me. That mission wasn't John's breakfast. Also, rightly or wrongly, I had taken the gun from the glove compartment and I could feel it nestling in a small pouch strapped to my waist.

Chapter Eleven

Janet's Journal

Instinctively, when we reached the outskirts of Guildford, we headed for the Cathedral. Not because it is a distinctive building as in most cities, or on high ground, but because it would be a natural place for the local population to meet. The centre of town could be dangerous with looters and there was not much on the higher ground at the Castle, which, let's face it, had been going downhill since they took the roof off in 1630. In a village the natural mustering point would be the village hall, the pub or the church. In larger places there might be several community halls and churches — perhaps fractured over Protestant, Catholic, Muslim and so on. What a wasted opportunity for some business rationalisation for someone to start a MegaPubRestaurantTakeaway dedicated to pagan feasting and a SuperChurchMosqueSynagogueTemple for multi-denominational worship.

What we found instead was disappointing. The Cathedral was virtually empty. There were a few waifs and strays huddled under blankets hiding in the bubble-shaped Lady Chapel at the head of the church but no sense of the central part of the building (ie. the altar and the nave) being used as a sanctuary. I wondered idly if the absence of traditional Gothic or Norman architecture with a tall spire piercing the sky made this comparatively modern building a less ingrained and instinctive place to assemble and seek refuge.

We spoke to the few people there. Some wouldn't respond, just grunted and turned their back. One person told us that they had come there from a really good building on an industrial estate. It belonged to one of the now defunct telecoms companies – Avaya he thought. We asked her why she had left. She told us that they had run out of food and there was fighting over what was left. Another person recommended a local leisure centre but we thought this was probably his idea of a joke – hiding from a flood in a place best known for it's large complex of swimming pools and wave machine. So, wearily, we decided not to explore further but to press on in the direction of London.

The light was beginning to fade again. There seemed to be a lot of dust in the air which was caught in the fading sunlight and made the sky glow with a warm iridescent orange. A giant marmalade cat smile. Cats, of course, don't smile. When they bear their teeth it is normally aggression or fear. I made a mental note not to smile at the cat in the sky, not with bare teeth anyway. If you want to smile at a cat, I was once told, then you have to narrow or close your eyes. It was beautiful and quiet whatever that presaged or perhaps it should be 'post-aged' as it was after a new start had been delivered and paid for. A neon afterglow undisturbed by headlights and traffic noise. Like an African sunset from the Maasai Mara. We found a suitably flat topped tree standing defiantly on its own under which to make camp. All the lower branches under the water line must have been broken off by debris. Whilst on the outskirts of Guildford we had salvaged some tarpaulin and threw this over some torn stumps from the tree's previous companions and tied it off as high as we could around the trunk of the remaining tree. There was some brief conversation, a small fire lit with a discarded cigarette lighter and a few soggy biscuits. Tired and sore, we communally decided it was time to go to sleep before sleep overtook us involuntarily.

Everyone slept soundly despite the odd rustle and distant thud during the night. It was a sleep without fear. A careless abandonment to fate. Since one of the worst things that could happen had already happened we, quite reasonably in my view, felt we had a right to some quiet time. My father had a saying which he would always trot out at the worst times, "if you think things are bad now they can always get worse." Thanks Dad. I wasn't my father and had no intention of living his aphorisms.

In the certainty of sleep the ship stood still. All around the cabin animals, vegetables and minerals flew by at 188 miles per second. Noah's Ark glowed in clever strategy and answers. You, too, know the answer... you just need to remember it. All twenty questions accelerated and reduced into clarity and simplicity. Gilbert and Charlie are playing with their bedroom toys and you are bursting with energy and ideas for the future. The white dove, the kingfisher rainbow, the choir of angels. But as soon as you wake it becomes confusing. Good morning.

It was an eerily quiet morning. Not a breath of wind. We were becalmed and didn't really know which direction we were travelling in. We wanted to head into the East but, although it was daytime, there wasn't an obvious point of light. The sky was a grey blanket and that's how the damp ground looked – a grey reflective sludge robbed of life. I longed to see a familiar face, any familiar face, just walk up to me in a bright scarlet coat, blue trainers and oversize canary yellow jumper. The coloured lights and life of humanity seemed to have been washed out at too high a temperature and all the usual colour, noise and vibrancy had gone down the drain. It was just an illusion, a cruel joke. I guess that was why we had agreed to head off back to the metropolis in the forlorn hope that if there was life resisting, fighting back, making a noise, then surely it would be there. Then an awful thought – what if we got there, what if we spent the last of our energy trying to get there, and when we finally collapsed, gasping at the centre of London – say Trafalgar Square, scene of so many communal celebrations of optimism – there was nothing. Just nothing.

Then I realised. If we got there and we thought there was nothing, then we couldn't be more wrong. It would no longer be nothing. We would be there, full of hope and optimism. Misplaced perhaps. Short-lived even. But something would exist. We would exist. We would be living and able to realise that we had been hurtling through time and place. We had survived the journey so far and had so much to tell anyone who would listen. Wherever it was and whenever it was. It didn't matter. It was time to hurry on and not worry about the future. I woke the others. "Quickly," I said, "time to go."

Chapter Twelve

That's where it ended. At least the journal did. Marking the page was a postcard of Trafalgar Square. On the back was scrawled the phrase, 'Rex Me Fecit'. It was a phrase I had seen before on ancient artefacts and simply meant 'the King made me' implying royal patronage for whatever had been done. But it also implied, to me anyway, a sense of compulsion: that the King made me do it. There was no indication that the craftsman had been willing. He or she surely wouldn't have wanted to mark a beautiful object with the graffiti that someone else had made it when they clearly hadn't.

So did she get to Trafalgar Square? Did she experience any kind of apotheosis there or great existential revelation? Did she remember what she thought she needed to, when she was asleep on the ark? I needed to ask Janet what happened next. Or did nothing happen? Was it just dull platitudes issued from a drug addled brain? It seemed crazy to me that we were stumbling about when there was one person who could give us a straight answer. But the surreal juxtapositions and dreamlike nature of much of the journal probably meant that the answer would be equally cryptic. Did Janet know, or was she just compelled as if being swept along by the flood water? Maybe it wasn't a thing but a person, or a set of people, she felt powerless to resist. The King, the government, the company?

I must have dropped off with these questions because I was woken by what must have been a doorbell followed by a loud knocking on the door. I tried to rub the sleep out of my eyes and shake the stiffness out of my limbs and sore neck where I had slumped to one side in the armchair.

I opened the door before I thought about whether it was safe to open the door. But there was no-one there. It was starting to get light. The last time I'd been awake at this time of day there were still milk deliveries. Instinctively I looked down. There was a plastic box. Again I opened it without thinking "this might be a bomb!" It wasn't a bomb, it was sausages. And underneath there were rashers of bacon, a tin of Italian peeled plum tomatoes, a tin of baked beans, a carton of eggs and a note. I opened the note and it read in big capital letters, 'HEAT THEN EAT, XXX S.'

"Thanks Suzanne, I really needed those instructions. I was going to eat the sausages raw."

Then I also thought, "Shit, I never logged in and deleted that data."

Suzanne didn't care. She was a long way from the van sitting on a train to the north east of Scotland. Janet wasn't in Wales – that was just what she had told the others. She just came up with the first place she thought of, that sounded a bit like Aberdeen as she started to say it, and that was Aberystwyth.

She had told Suzanne that she was going to see Stella Maris. The name meant nothing to Suzanne but she knew what train ticket she'd booked because she saw the confirmation page left up on Janet's laptop. She asked Phe if she knew a Stella that might be a friend of Janet's and lived in Wales or, more likely, Scotland. Phe laughed and said you need to look to the stars... to the Star of the Sea. Phe knew that Janet was a Catholic... or at least a lapsed Catholic... or at least had one Catholic parent and enough of an early Sunday Schooling to know some saints and myths. She also knew, from singing shanties with the locals in seaside folk clubs, about the Apostleship of the Sea which was an agency that gave pastoral care to seafarers in distress (although she wasn't entirely sure what pastoral care meant.) The vague idea of some sort of spiritual and physical refuge made perfect sense to Phe whilst it sounded odd to Suzanne who couldn't think that Janet would want to lean on a religion that she never admitted to having any interest in. Nothing she knew about Janet made sense of her recent words and actions but then nothing she knew about Janet made sense anyway.

Being on the train with not very much to do for a very long time gave Suzanne the chance to recollect her life with Janet. As she did so she found herself staring at the blur of the hedge line punctuated by sudden telegraph poles and gates and surrendering to the rhythm of the track joints and the slight roll of the bends.

She had been on a train once with Janet. Suzanne was frustrated that Janet's head was always turned towards the window. Her thick brown hair was shoulder length and curled up and bouncy at the neck of her plum cardigan. She seemed to want to see as much as she could from the train window as if travelling on a plane for the first time. Suzanne was bored. The countryside was boring. It was all flat and green. After all it wasn't as if they were travelling through Scotland, North Wales or the Lake District. They were on a branch line in the West Midlands. The boredom was punctuated by the odd town but mostly just nothing.

I remember, she thought, Janet turned to me and said, "Hey did you see that horse? I think it was one of the old plough horses. What do you call them? Shire, that's it. He had flared trousers like a seventies rock star!"

"How do you know it was a he? It could have been a female rock star."

"No this was definitely a he-horse. Those poor mares. God knows what he must be like when he gets excited."

"Really? Trust you to look. And how could you look anyway? We were past in a flash. You'd be lucky to register whether he had one head or two."

"No there was only one penis. Two would just be silly." She thought about it for a minute. "Unless you had it on your forehead. But I guess that could make eating grass awkward. You'd bang it on the floor every time you tried to eat. It would get very sore. You'd have to wear underpants on your head. You could get one ear in each leg hole but you'd have to cut extra holes for your eyes and I think that might be difficult because it's so hard to grip the scissors between your hooves."

I slapped her on the shoulder and told her not to be such an idiot. Then shuffled in towards her so that I could feel her hipbone against mine and briefly put my forehead on the rear of her shoulder.

Janet carried on looking out of the window. I looked down at her narrow legs primly angled together under the train table. She wore a modest pleated black skirt – they must have been popular at the time – and dark stockings. She was never over-dressed. That was my department. But she had a style she was comfortable with and that made you comfortable with her.

We could talk about anything, whether it was nonsense or raw heartfelt emotion and Janet would always have the level-headed good humour and common sense not to take things too seriously. She seemed to be able to take life in her stride. Even that awful family that got on at Dudley and insisted on sitting together and glaring at us to give up one of our two booked seats even though the kids were just running up and down the aisle shouting. Or that spotty teenager from Smethwick that you could hear every beat of the drum and bass from his ear pods and left spilt lager and crisp packets all over the red plastic table. Janet would just smile beatifically like Mary Poppins and sort it out with a handy tissue pack.

Janet was still watching the hedgerows, banks, trees, animals, buildings, vehicles and fences blurring past the window as if transfixed by a firework display or a psychedelic light show. Her concentration was fierce and intense. I asked her about what she wanted to eat this evening and what time she thought we might get back to the flat. She didn't hear me even though I asked twice. Then I pulled at her sleeve and she was back with me.

Later, when we were getting near home, I asked her what she had been thinking about on the journey. She said that she had spent as much time in China as Wolverhampton and that it had been a combination of walking and horseback but not rail.

I asked her if that was a tourist holiday she'd been remembering.

She said she was an Italian Jesuit priest.

That stalled me for a bit. But, trying to play along, I asked her if this was in the Nineteenth Century or some time past as that was when I had imagined Christian missionaries went into China.

No she said, it was 1601.

I asked her if she had seen some film or documentary about it.

She said no, she'd never seen anything, heard anything, ever thought about it. She didn't know why she said 1601 but when I looked it up on the internet she wasn't surprised that I found an Italian Jesuit priest called Matteo Ricci who established a mission in that year. She went on to tell me details about the journey but I couldn't substantiate any of these in relation to the history of this man Ricci.

At the time I didn't think anything more about it. She had obviously been told or heard about this and not consciously remembered. The rest she had imagined.

But now, sitting on the train and staring out of the window, it seemed entirely natural. It seemed part of Janet's nature to travel in her mind anywhere she wanted or perhaps didn't want. I don't suppose she could control it any more than I could really control the fact that I was thinking about her now. Wasn't that the same thing? I was travelling to Aberdeen and yet in my mind I was on the outskirts of Wolverhampton nearly a decade ago, being a young student on a train and snuggling up to Janet.

Time to change at Edinburgh according to the train announcement. God this is a long journey. I half expected to have arrived in a different city and at a different time. I thought maybe everybody would be wearing strange masks and I would be transferred on to a Venetian gondola in the hot evening light. No such luck. That would have been my choice but this was definitely Edinburgh Waverley on a cool, damp, overcast day in the twenty first century. I needed a third coffee and something to read. Actually it was quite a nice station as stations go and in better weather I would have been happy to explore or re-explore the city. But the train from Birmingham was running a bit late and I wanted to make sure of the connection. Otherwise I would have spent at least a night and a day here but that wasn't why I'd come.

Mark wiped the sleep from his eyes as he blundered into the kitchen. "I see Suzanne kept her promise – I could smell it from upstairs." Mark's timing was good as the cooked breakfast was being plated up.

"Sort of," John replied. "She delivered but I cooked."

"Ah well, she probably deserves a break. Is she sleeping it off?"

"No idea."

Mark took up position seated at the kitchen table, grabbing his knife and fork firmly in each fist, banging them on the table upright and ready for action. I had prepared three plates and put one of them on the table for Mark with a side plate of toast. Mark greedily set to work. I put one of the plates I'd prepared under the grill to keep warm and then sat down with my own meal at the table. We sat eating together in noisy silence.

It was only after a little while Mark asked, "Where's Suzanne? Had you better call her?"

"No she's not here."

"Sorry?"

"She only came back to deliver the food, or at least I assume she had. I guess she could have had it delivered. It was probably her, it certainly came with one of her sarcy notes."

"What?" Mark shouted, spluttering baked bean sauce over the far reaches of the table.

He got up, twisted this way and that as if some urgent action was needed.

"I knew I shouldn't have left you in charge. Have you any idea where she is?"

"None at all. Have you any idea where Hugh is?" I countered.

"Yes, he's gone to Scotland." Mark answered instantly, then regretted saying anything and wouldn't be drawn further. After a few moment's indecision he seemed to calm down and sat down although not to eat.

"Tell me again," he asked breathing deeply, "what you think Suzanne said or did and where she might be."

"There's not a lot to tell. She set off with the van, as you know, and I didn't hear back from her. I was tired and fell asleep. There was a noise at the door. It was dawn, more or less in the early light anyway. I answered but there was no-one there, just a box of food with a note from Suzanne telling me to cook it myself. Only one more thing …I'm afraid I forgot to try and sabotage the vehicle tracking."

"Fuck." Mark got up again and left the room.

I guess that was the end of breakfast. I threw the unused food, including the third plate, in the bin and started washing up.

Chapter Thirteen

Hugh was on his way north. Not by train. He was driving a lemon coloured Citroen. He had been tipped off by Phe and he had a good start on Suzanne. But he was not a fast traveller and, as well as keeping his speed down, he also wanted to keep his rest periods up. He had planned to travel over three days stopping at anonymous cheap hotels or motels for breakfast, lunch, supper and fitful sleep. This involved long evenings sat with a single half of lager reading, thinking and ignoring people.

What he was reading – and there were normally six or seven books or journals on his table – was about the brain and about memory. He was fascinated by everything he knew and experienced being dictated by a bunch of organs, tissues and nerves exchanging electrical and chemical communication. But it wasn't simply the fact that these thoughts and experiences far surpassed in subtlety and mysterious complexity anything that could so far be engineered with metal and wire. What really fascinated him was the fact that his brain was lying to him.

He knew that you could deceive the eyes. As a student he had taken part in class experiments where you would stare at an image – say a red spot on a sheet of paper and then when you exchanged it for a blank sheet of paper you would still have a residual image of the spot for a few seconds. Sometimes it wasn't even the same colour, just the same shape. He knew colours were subjective – that many humans and most animal and insect eyes all perceived them slightly differently. Most of the class assumed the spot test was the brain being lazy and slow to catch up with what was really happening. Hugh had the opposite thought, that the brain was being proactive and predicting what was going to happen in the future but that sometimes it got it wrong.

With one eye on a career in sport physiology and psychology he had done some studies for a thesis on sporting action. It interested him that some of the best performers seemed to catch or predict motion faster than the human eye. He got some funding for it from a football club hoping to improve their record on saving penalties. In fact Hugh's studies were statistically useless for goalkeepers as they couldn't translate the data into a more meaningful algorithm of probability than they already had. What it did seem to prove was that human perception of motion is slightly ahead of time. In the same way the brain quickly fills in the dots of facial recognition from partial information, ie. that an eye, nose and lips belongs to the rest of a face and therefore a person. It does the same with time. The brain assumes that a car is moving in a particular direction from the slightest blur and that another is stationary. It does these probability calculations a thousand times with all sorts of objects from the merest glance. But Hugh didn't trust his brain to get it right which is why he drove very slowly and admired scientists who had worked on pedestrian impact and collision calculations for self-driving cars.

On the whole he thought the human eye/brain combination was pretty smart on environmental perception though not perfect. But the thing that most confused him about the brain was the memory function. On the table in front of him was a medical journal that had interviewed a number of people after a traumatic event – a terrorist incident. The testimonies were detailed and included meaningless information about colour, places and paraphrased speech. The same test subjects were interviewed one and two years later. The results astounded Hugh. Over 50% had changed details between the direct experience at the time and the subsequent interview. Some of these changes were substantial including where they were and who they were with. On the third interview there were less changes, barely any substantial ones, but there were still some changes even between couples that had had the same experience. The memories were still evolving and being refined into a different narrative and the individuals were adamant they were right and remembered the incident correctly.

Hugh had experienced things that quickly disappear from short term or what he liked to call his flash memory. But he wasn't expecting long term memories to be so fickle.

He could understand how you could misfile a memory and find it hard to recall without the right trigger or index or metadata. But all these individuals were given access to the right context and they were telling the truth as they believed it, even when, objectively, it could be disproved to them.

When confronted with these changes people couldn't understand and often flatly denied the accuracy of the original transcript from the incident. Their brains, which is after all the essence of who they were, were continuing to lie to them. Hugh wanted to know why and, also, how.

Suzanne also wanted answers and although, from previous experience, Janet couldn't or wouldn't want to explain, she felt that Mark and John were lost in some boy's game of industrial espionage and were missing the real point. For her it was always, and purely, saving Janet from whatever was making her ill. What had brought her here to this eastern coast of Scotland? Looking from the train window Suzanne could only see cloud and spray. It must be stunning on a nice day she thought. But how often would it be a nice day? Sometimes, of course, but not today. It was also flatter than she was expecting. She must have thought she was going to the Cairngorms and had been looking forward to this leg of the journey from Edinburgh to Aberdeen. As it was she was tired, tired of the train, tired of the rain, tired of being cold and hungry. There was supposed to be a food and drink trolley but there had been some mix-up and it was being put on at a later station. So she sat, looking out of the window at the occasional objects that would whizz by, barely perceived, through the fogged up windows.

Now she was going over a bridge – a seemingly endless one – metal girders providing a syncopated rhythm, kerdunking between lengths of track. It was curiously soothing, like a mother humming to an infant.

When Suzanne looked up the train had stopped. That must be what had woken her. The silence.

Somebody was shouting in the next carriage. It was getting louder, more insistent. The door burst open and a Japanese officer approached Suzanne. He was shouting at her. Something she couldn't understand. He grabbed her roughly by one shoulder and dragged and pushed her through the carriageway to the nearest door. Suzanne saw a flash of green undergrowth and was then thrown through the door and onto the tracks. Someone was laughing. Suzanne could taste the hot humid earth and clinker. She felt as if she was boiling up and although sweating, her throat was achingly dry. Someone, maybe the laughing one, hit her across the back of the head with a wooden or metal object. They barked something in a sort of English. She couldn't catch what they said. Suzanne turned her sore head to see who had struck her. The sky was now a vivid blue and it was a young sweaty black-haired man with a stick in a filthy but different uniform to the one on the train.

"Are you Japanese?" she asked, trying to orientate herself.

He laughed again. "Korean interpreter. You go there." He pointed. "Welcome to Siam."

Geography was one of Suzanne's most hated subjects at school, followed swiftly by history, mathematics, science, English and cookery, but she was pretty sure that Siam didn't exist anymore.

"Kanchanaburi," someone behind her further explained in an Australian accent, "where the Khwae Noi and Khwae Yai rivers meet the Mae Klong river. Your job is to finish the bridge. Then you can rest."

The Korean laughed again.

Well at least he enjoyed his work.

Then he beat the person who had spoken down to his knees.

It didn't take much. He looked half-starved anyway. He had a pair of baggy canvas shorts and the remains of a shirt that seemed to merge with the skin on his back, around a bony ribcage as stark in its angles as the metal supports on the bridge onto which he had collapsed.

Suzanne painfully turned her head towards the riverbank. It was a deep vivid green totally unlike the washed out greens, greys and browns she'd seen on the journey so far.

And it was so hot, the insects stung and she didn't have the energy to wave them away.

"Damn these Scottish midges" she thought, "I'd been told they were bad but this is unbearable." The weather must have cleared quickly, leaving a steaming wet brightness.

There were a gaggle of people at the other end of the bridge. She hadn't seen them before, but an unsynchronised tapping sound was echoing down the rudimentary track. Then she heard the scraping and more shouting which she thought at first was the yapping and growling of a set of dogs but realised was human. It wasn't insistent and energetic, but tired and lazy, as if they felt they should be shouting and were struggling to keep it up.

Now that Suzanne could focus through the haze she saw the gangs were separated into two groups – some pale and some dark that seemed better dressed in flappy shorts/skirts and loose towels around their heads. The Korean interpreter seemed to be distracted by following the Japanese officer so she ventured to ask the Australian who the other gang were.

"Tamils," he said, "nice fellas but worse off than us."

Then the Korean had returned, took an idle swipe at the Australian who had only just got back to his feet, and ushered them down the track to join the rest of the white gang. I say 'down the track', but, in truth, it was only half-built with piles of sleepers at the side. Only the bridge was complete.

Suzanne was set to work hitting something. She wasn't quite sure what or why. She was thirsty and felt weak. Someone was shouting at her. She made out the words 'death', a click and then 'railway' being repeated like the passage of a train over points. Then she realised it was 'deaf' and 'ticket' and 'railway'.

She looked up and there was sour faced red nosed man with spectacles and spots looming over her in a threatening way. He was saying something in what sounded like a foreign language but she could still make out, "so you're no deaf?" with the 'deaf' stretched out like 'deeeeeeef'. Suzanne couldn't find her ticket, she went through every pocket and bag then back through every pocket and bag then found it stuck with sweaty moisture onto the back of her phone. She offered it up silently, apologetically. There was a scowl and the man disappeared.

"Just a stupid dream then," she thought to herself. "What were the names of those rivers, I can't remember them now, Quai something and Me Klong?" Suzanne googled them. Quai just came up with quay or dock but she found Mae Klong or Maeklong easily enough after skipping over Mekong. Where would she have thought of that name? That's what puzzled Suzanne. Not the fact that she was now cold and covered in sweat; not the fact that everywhere outside the train was dripping with moisture and yet her throat was dry. Those effects of the variation in temperature and atmosphere were easily explained with the vagaries of 'blast or bust' heating systems and draughts through open and closed doors on a train. Then she noticed she also had dirt under her fingernails. She found her compact mirror. Her hair was a mess. So what, but she also had smears of black dirt on her face. Maybe the carriage was filthy. She looked under the table. There was a sweet wrapper and a free newspaper but on the whole it was pretty clean.

She stumbled along to the toilet, banging against the tops of seats as she was feeling a little unsteady and her muscles ached. She cleaned herself up as best she could and had no time for further reflection as she heard over the tannoy system that she was approaching her final destination.

"All services terminate here."

She reminded herself that this was where she would find Janet, and Janet would hopefully be the end of this journey or the start of a new one. She asked herself if they were both the same thing but didn't really mind as long as she could find her.

Suzanne was relieved to get out and see the wide expanse of smooth station floor topped by steel framed glass roof. There were not many people around but the familiar Victorian architecture gave Suzanne a sense of comfort and coming home. She found some hot greasy comfort food and when she'd wiped her fingers down on her skirt went to find the taxi rank.

She had phoned ahead, and was expected, but she hadn't given her real name and was posing as a confused and vulnerable traveller with a problem past. After all, she told herself, she didn't need to act the part. She felt this was her true self even without reference to the Sue who had led spies through a park, attacked security guards and hid their van.

The taxi had dropped her on the wrong side of a dual carriageway by the docks. She could just see the tops of distant ships as she crossed but the foreground was blocked by industrial warehouses.

Her target destination, where she now stood, was an ordinary grey Victorian house with shop style glass windows full of posters of welcome about help lines but with unwelcoming double wooden doors that were firmly shut and locked. She knew because she tried them, and knocked, before she eventually saw and pressed the little buzzer.

There was a long wait.

She pressed again.

She started to wander up the street to see if there was a back entrance when she noticed that one of the blue doors was now slightly ajar.

She walked back and opened it.

It clicked shut behind her.

There was no-one there in the corridor. Perhaps it was opened and closed remotely.

Wandering along the corridor there were a set of small offices to either side with whitewashed windows. There was an over-powering smell of paint, disinfectant and something else. Fish? No, she must be imagining it.

Past the offices the corridor led out onto a small lounge with plastic sofas and a coffee table and a scattered pile of magazines whose covers mostly featured cheery middle-aged men in hard hats and Hi-Vis in front of winching gear.

There were a couple of young men already sitting there staring into the middle distance.

Suzanne tried to engage them in conversation but it was painfully clear they had no English. But at least they had a friendly smile and seemed relaxed. One of them had lost most of his fingers… but not recently, thank goodness.

Suzanne sat and waited. Presumably it was some sort of waiting area and somebody would be along in a minute.

They weren't.

Strangely Suzanne didn't mind. It felt like some sort of sanctuary, some sort of refuge. But she wasn't quite sure what she was running from. She hadn't come here to get away but to move forward. She wanted to hit some kind of reset button on her life, to start as a different person, hopefully with Janet.

Chapter Fourteen

"The Chaplain will see you now."

I awoke from my reverie to find a short ruddy faced woman speaking to me. The two young men had gone. I hadn't seen them go.

I followed her down another corridor, deeper into the centre of the building. There were more offices, also with whitewashed windows and god knows what going on behind them. I was ushered into what seemed to be the smallest one at the end. The lady asked, "Do you want a coffee dear?"

"Yes," I replied before I realised she wasn't talking to me. There was a handsome youngish man sitting at a desk in the office who said, "Yes please, two. White without?" He asked looking at me. I nodded. I realised he had made eye contact with me whereas the lady hadn't. He had arresting pale blue eyes. There was a touch of greying around the ears but otherwise he had clear straw-coloured hair. He was wearing a brilliant white plain t-shirt and jeans that were ironed with a strong central crease down the legs (or at least the one I could see around the side of the desk) as if he would have been more comfortable in a suit but had been forced to dress down for work.

"Sit down Suzanne," he said.

I must have gawped with my mouth open. How the hell did he know my real name. He laughed at my unspoken question.

I chose a chair. There were two. There wouldn't have been room for any more. God knows how they got the desk in. Must have assembled it in the room from a kit I guess.

He didn't say anything more.

It was clearly my turn first. Was this going to be a confessional? With deliberate effort I dragged up the story I had prepared and it all tumbled out like throwing all my childhood toys down the stairs.

I was an orphan – sounded fine when I prepared it but when spoken out loud it sounded like the beginning of a long line of clichés that I was ill-prepared to substantiate. I had left care at 16 and drifted to Bristol and on from there to Cardiff and a casual job doing silver service on a cruise ship. I had some bad experiences. Bullying and sexual harassment which triggered earlier memories, that I thought I had buried, of what had happened to me and others in care – as I was speaking I made a mental note that I must dance lightly over these childhood stories as I don't have any real experience or emotional depth to explain them authentically. Should I add drug use? Probably not, as I didn't have the vernacular to describe which drugs would be most popular with a bored but poor ship's crew and how they would be taken. I told him I got into trouble with the head steward as I dropped some hot soup over our most important guest. It was on purpose. He'd made some stupid remark about bunking up with him after the meal. I knew he was just playing to the rest of the crowd at the table, and probably wasn't serious, but it was just a final straw when the rest started egging him on and cheering. I was wearing a see-through white blouse and short black skirt that the company insisted on us wearing for formal dinners. He kept doing things like asking me to lean over him to pass the salt then moving it further away. I reacted instinctively and overturned a handy tureen of the hot stuff into his lap. I was dropped off at the nearest port. The contract (what contract?) was severed. No money. I was in South America and no way of getting home. Rather than drift into drug use and prostitution the only other option was to stow aboard a ship. I soon found this was not as easy as I'd hoped. After a few harrowing experiences I managed to get a kitchen job on a cargo ship and ended up in Aberdeen. The head cook was a psychopath who used to kick me and shout for no apparent reason when under stress, which was most of the time, but otherwise he and the rest of the kitchen staff let me be.

The man sitting opposite – I think the lady who briefly returned with the coffees called him Doug – said nothing.

I wondered whether I should invent some more but wasn't sure he believed anything I had said so far anyway so I just stayed silent.

Eventually he looked up, as if realising the time, and said, "Well you can't stay here. We have limited accommodation and that's mostly taken up with the injured and threatened."

Obviously I belonged to some lower category like 'self-inflicted idiot with minor talent for being too pathetic to sort my own life out'. Maybe I should have laid it on a bit more strongly with the drugs after all.

He was looking at my hands and guessing they were pretty soft and unused to manual labour. It's true I hadn't pulled any winches lately but I didn't think I'd necessarily get calluses from gutting fish, opening tins and doing the washing up. Anyway I quickly folded my hands on my lap below the desk line.

He thought a bit longer. "There is someone I can put you with. They're not a regular. Just an occasional volunteer but they could do with some company. Maybe I can persuade them to take you for a week or two."

I didn't know what to say. I knew I should be grateful but this isn't quite what I'd imagined. I was hoping we would be in some communal centre with bunk beds and all have our meals together so I could bump into Janet.

I think he noticed that I didn't look too keen so I added an unnecessary, but slightly muttered, "that would be great, if you could."

He left the room, presumably to make a phone call.

Eventually he returned with a bunch of paperwork which he left with me and went off again. He didn't say anything about the placement so I guessed it was either going through but not yet finalised or maybe he just hadn't been able to get in touch.

The forms were a bit difficult. There were a few things on there they could easily check and find out were false. Particularly as I was forced to use my real name. Apparently, I'd given it to the taxi driver who just happened to be a part time volunteer at the centre and who had innocently sent a text to them when he dropped me off. So I had to take the chance that the organisation was just paper driven by habit and liked to collect useless information, rather than they were going to do anything with it in terms of cross-checking.

I wondered how some of the non-English speakers would deal with these forms. I found them difficult enough. Who can quote off the top of their head their UK National Insurance number?

I was still waiting after what seemed an hour. I felt my mind drifting back to the South American sea voyage that I never had, remembering incidents and faces that never existed, the feeling of sea sickness was suddenly overwhelming. That scared me. I had to get up. I stumbled along the corridor. Someone spoke but it was distant and distorted. I could barely see. I pushed the front door open after bashing it a few times and realising there was a release button to the left on the wall.

The cold air hit me like a heavyweight boxer. I doubled over and was sick on the pavement. Bye-bye sausage roll and pasty. But the retching wouldn't stop even though there was nothing left. I knelt in abject heaving misery surrounded by a pool of chunky vomit. Carrots anyone? Of course the pavement was slightly sloping back towards me and my stocking knees were starting to soak in it. Puddled and stinking. The smell set me off dry retching and hurting my raw throat again.

I noticed there were a pair of hands holding my shoulders. I glanced sideways, not wanting whoever it was to see my face. It was Doug. He'd come out onto the pavement and was just gently squatted down to lightly hold me, reassure me, just to be there for me and to stop me from collapsing face first in the slime.

"I'm sorry. It was a long journey and I'm not feeling too good."

"Come back in and have a glass of water. When you're ready. There's no hurry."

He let go of my shoulders.

I really wished he hadn't but I guess he suddenly remembered that he had to be careful about physical contact with his clients — particularly after my tales of harassment. Too many accusations of priests and other so-called carers taking advantage of vulnerable people. Having his arms resting on my back and his strong hands on my shoulders seemed to anchor me though and bring me back to the here and now. Otherwise I might have drifted off into some storm and sunk beneath the waves. That's how it felt. Something powerful and malevolent trying to batter me and drag me under. It also brought back the experience on the bridge and, despite the cold city air, I felt the alternately cold and hot tropical sweats. I knew that my face and neck was flushed with throbbing strawberry embarrassment. I must look a total mess but I really didn't care. This was about survival. I didn't want to go back to the death railway. I needed to stay here. To hide. To be locked in. I wanted to be in bed and to hide in Davy Jones' locker and sweat it out under the blankets.

I felt so useless. Without strength. At least without any strength in my limbs. But, counterintuitively, it also made my resolve firmer than ever. I would find Janet. We would make things right. Make things safe.

"I'm ready now," I told Doug. He helped me up and into the Gents. Why the Gents? I don't know. Perhaps he felt more comfortable in there. There was a glass of water. I don't know where that came from but after wiping my face with toilet paper and taking a glance in the mirror, which I regretted, I sipped from the glass. Then sipped again. Then sipped again. Then drank it down.

Doug offered to get anything I needed from my handbag. I said yes then panicked and grabbed his arms really hard as I realised I still had the gun from the black van in there.

"No, no, no, it's alright, I'll be fine."

Slowly I let go of his arms. He looked at me quizzically and when I stared back he was all meekness like a frightened rabbit.

Then I washed my face properly with liquid soap and water as Doug knelt by my side and brushed the worst off my knees with some tissue paper. It wasn't very effective and left slivers of toilet paper up and down my clothes but I was grateful and he looked less frightened of me now.

He asked me if I wanted to go to the toilet. I didn't, or at least I said I didn't, so he helped me back out to the lounge. It was empty and I sat down clutching my second, half full, glass of water as if it would float away like a helium balloon if I didn't grasp it really tightly.

Doug disappeared.

I wondered where the other lady was or any of the office workers and clients.

Then I realised it was late afternoon coming on to early evening and how quickly these sort of places empty out of people working in the public and voluntary sectors.

Doug reappeared, clutching the pile of paperwork and said, "It's all settled. Irene will take you. I'll drive you there now."

He had a marked parking space around the back. Just a small average car. Nothing flash. The journey was barely ten minutes long and most of that was stationary at traffic lights. But I noticed that Doug's attitude had changed. Whereas, right from the get go, he had seemed aloof, contemptuous of my taking his time, not treating me like a genuine victim which, after all, was fair enough as I wasn't. Now he was now very conciliatory, very caring. I knew he was just being his professional self and would have treated any human being well who appeared to need help but, at that time and place, I was glad to be that human being and get that professional help.

So I was accepted in to the refuge or hospice or whatever it was. I hoped he didn't think I'd staged the illness or was pulling some sort of dizzy blonde maiden in distress act. Of course not. No-one could act that well. I still felt pretty wobbly and totally drained.

Frankly, at the moment, I didn't care what anybody thought.

I just needed time to rest and to rethink. I wanted to press a reset button on my life.

Curiously pretending to be someone else, somewhere else, felt like a way of cleansing my pride and my past and offered me the opportunity to take time to consider who I was, where I wanted to be and with whom.

Chapter Fifteen

I could hear Mark getting dressed and shaved upstairs. I was in a bit of a mood and felt useless. Situation normal some might say.

I didn't know what to do. Hopefully Mark would have a plan. He was the man of action.

He came downstairs and the first thing he said was. "I don't know what to do." He slumped down on one of the chairs. So much for the man of action.

"Should we try to get her back?" I asked.

"How?"

"Phone her and ask her?"

"I don't have her number."

"What?" Then I realised I didn't either.

"How did you organise all those meetings? You phoned me."

"With Suzanne it was always verbal. Pre-arranged dates, times and places. That was part of the thing. A bit cloak and dagger. Dead letter drops. You know."

I didn't. "Great," I said.

"We're stuck then."

"Not exactly. I know where she is but I don't think it would be a good idea to go there."

"How do you know where she is when half an hour ago you were surprised she wasn't here?"

"I know where Janet is and my guess is Suzanne will go there... sooner or later. Even though we agreed not to. The whole idea was to give Janet the time and space to do her thing. We were just a distraction to her recovery."

"What do you mean? You are talking in riddles again. Am I involved in this or not? You just tell me what you think I need to know. Which is bugger all. Suzanne was the same."

"Oh you're up to your eyes in it alright. Don't worry about that John."

"So... tell me everything or tell me to bugger off."

"There's not a lot to tell. That's Suzanne's job. She was supposed to be giving you the back story."

"What do you mean 'the back story'? Why do I feel like I'm in some sort of set up, some practical joke and I'm going to find myself laughed at on light entertainment TV? Surely Janet was the one with the back story with her weirdy journal."

"Well yes, I guess you're right. The back story is Janet's. But she wasn't in any fit state to tell it cogently. That's the point. We needed someone more objective to interpret it and make sense of it from our perspective. Suzanne felt she understood it, or at least part of it. She couldn't work out what was going on at the company. Now she's gone and she's the only one likely to get anything out of Janet."

"What about Phe?"

"What?"

"What about Phe? What's her role in this fiasco and can she help? Is she worth going to see now?"

"I don't know. It's not a totally disastrous idea though. Phe knows nothing about the company but she knows Janet and I think she probably understands her better than Hugh does. I must admit all I could think of was going back to Harman and trying to wreck whatever is going on there. We have the access. You have the IT security, I have the physical security. We could get in and totally destroy everything. That was my idea."

"You call that an idea. Is Harman full of evil masterminds conspiring to take over the planet? I think I'd like to see some pretty strong evidence of wrongdoing before I wanted to destroy it, even if I could."

"Well perhaps we could get in and get the evidence."

"I don't like it. Fiddling a bread crumb trail to make it harder to find the van is one thing but I'd need something a lot stronger to bite the hand that's fed me, let's face it, pretty well over the last few years; even though I don't expect I'll ever be able to work there again. Besides there are bigger concerns for me. One is doing something illegal for which I could be imprisoned. The second is a bit more prosaic but very important to me. I need a reference for Christ's sake! How do you think I'm going to get another job? Also what the hell would I be looking for anyway if we did go there?"

"Janet's personnel file would be a good place to start."

"Are you kidding? Have you been to our HR department? The records are all over the place. Some paper, some archived, some in one system, some in another. Training records and disciplinary records kept separately from everything else. Three different performance systems as we keep changing them and failing to migrate the data properly. The department and staff records have grown organically as we acquired different companies, with different data stores, and it was never consolidated. Besides, when you find a record, you'll be lucky if it's anything other than a name (likely misspelt after a marriage or divorce), staff number and date of birth. Forget psychological profiling."

"Okay let's go see Phe then."

That was when we realised we didn't have any transport or know where Phe lived.

Another lengthy silence. Then we looked at each other and just laughed. For the first time I thought Mark is alright. He's not such a bear with a sore head. He's just clueless like me.

Then I had another idea. Two in one day. I should probably sit down and take a rest.

"I think I know how to find Phe. She plays in a band called Drogheda, or something like that, and I think they have some gigs coming up. They are bound to be advertised. She said they also play some folk club pretty much every week or, if not, co-ordinate some sort of open mike night where some of the band members just jam with whoever turns up. I'll do some searches. If you can sort out the transport I think we'll be in business. Can you hot wire a stolen car?"

Mark spluttered, "Yes I could, Mr. Hotshot, but I'd rather rent. Just as easy and less likely to attract attention. That reminds me, I should tell you more about Phe that she probably hasn't mentioned to you and that does link her to the company."

I looked at him quizzically.

Mark took a deep breath and then continued, "She has built up a bit of a reputation as a Celtic mystic. That was what attracted the attention of Harman. Some music fan in the office commissioned her to write music and lyrics around the pre-existing stories they had as game scenarios. It was for a project they were codenaming Rhiannon. That was how Phe met Janet again after knowing her at school. Janet didn't commission the work directly, but she was the handling the game scenarios and was invited to use whatever Phe came up with. It quickly became obvious to Janet that Harman had no idea what they meant by "Celtic". They had asked an Irish writer to write material for a project codenamed after a Welsh goddess associated with horses and the sea but the guideline brief from the company kept making references to Asterix and the Gauls beating up the Romans."

"That figures."

"Phe, bless her, tried her best. She justified it by saying that that they were right, in a sense, and that there have always been plenty of touchpoints between the cultures of this part of Europe. But in reality they were clearly after making some sort of Disney-style soup with standard fight and chase action that didn't fit well with Phe's experience and taste for darker and more obscure pacifist mysticism rooted in very specific places. Phe wrote them stories associated with a well or a stone in an individual map location in a field rather than some generic international hero figures."

"You obviously know Phe better than I do. You must know her band."

"No, not really. Anyway, the company never used any of her material and she was eventually asked to withdraw from the project. Janet kept in touch. I think she was trying to customise the project, whatever it was, in another direction."

"Does Phe know what direction?"

"No, I've asked her again and again. She wasn't really privy to what Harman wanted the material for and Janet didn't say. She just noticed the very modest payments she was getting started coming from a different bank account that turned out to be a personal account owned by Janet. But the payments dried up after a couple of months and Phe lost interest. By that time Janet was already starting to get sick."

"Has Phe seen Janet's Journal?"

"No, but Suzanne said it wasn't relevant."

"How does she know?"

"I don't know."

A quick search on the Drogheda band page, plus a bit of social media follow up, and I had a date and location in Bristol four days hence. It would have to do. There was a Messenger and email contact for the band but I didn't want to use it. I needed to eyeball Phe and talk to her and it could wait.

Mark sorted the hire car. A few phone calls and an agreement to pick up later that afternoon. I asked him if he was going to use his real name and ID. He said, "Yes of course. Why not? I'm just renting a car. I'm not intending to use it in a ram raid. Not intentionally anyway."

I had a sinking feeling that the car would get wrecked in some James Bond style car chase but maybe that was just me. After all we were just going to go to a gig in Bristol. What could possibly go wrong?

Nothing, as it happened. We booked into a cheap hotel. I fancied booking in as "Smith and Smith" and paying cash but Mark insisted on using real names again. So we spent a pleasant few days doing nothing very much. Mooching around the shops and trying to find Mark a Gym and a park he could run around in.

We arrived at the venue early as the doors were opening at 7pm. The main room was locked and all we had access to was a bar. Well, when in Bristol. So we had a couple of pints and settled down to wait. After half an hour or so Mark started to get a bit restless and suggested having a look around the back of the venue in case there was a rear entrance or he could see a tour bus arrive with the band and equipment. I reminded him that this was a folk group and they would probably turn up individually in a Morris Minor, or similar, with a violin case. Nonetheless he said he needed a pee and I knew he would be straight out of the gents and round the back trying to find 'the green room' or wherever it was that artists mysteriously appear from at venues without mingling with the punters.

More fool him as I think I recognised one of the band come into the bar with another bloke that I'd seen bossing the bar staff around earlier. He looked to me like an estate agent rather than a folk musician in terms of his hair style but the paisley shirt together with conspicuous earpieces and radio receiver strapped to his waist gave it away that he was dressed for audio action. Perhaps I was wrong about the professionalism of this band. I was thinking we would be lucky if they used a mike – I imagined us all huddled in a singing circle with one finger in our ears to help us keep in tune. That was just my clichéd stereotyped view of traditional folk music. Then I started to think about secret operatives and whether they would have earpieces. Then instantly dismissed the thought because this guy wasn't hiding any of the equipment he was wearing. A long-haired engineer then came up to him and started fiddling with the receiver on his waist. The guy at the bar was completely oblivious – or at least he must have glanced at him but then carried on speaking to the person from the venue.

I wondered whether I should approach him now or wait until I saw Phe. I hadn't really thought about it before but wondered whether I should have some sort of cover story because I imagined the reaction if I said to him, "We lost someone called Janet and hoped that someone called Suzanne could help us but we lost her too. We'd met Phe but then we lost her as well and haven't been able to find her. So we were hoping that Phe might be able to tell us where Suzanne was so that she could find Janet." The best scenario was that I'd just get puzzled blank looks before they turned around and carried on with their conversation. Worst was fetching the bouncer to introduce my face to the pavement outside the front door.

'Casual with confidence' advised my better self. So I drained what was left of my pint, went to the bar as if to order another but instead walked past the two of them turning as I do so to ask the musician simply, "Where's Phe?"

There was a slightly puzzled look on his face as if he was trying to hide the fact that he couldn't recall who I was but he said, "Through the door on the left talking to someone."

So I took the door on the left. It wasn't locked but it was marked Staff Only.

Phe was in there talking to Mark.

Phe looked up. Her broad smile was such a welcoming and reassuring sight.

"Hello John, are you going to stick around for the gig?"

"Absolutely – looking forward to it."

"Mark tells me you've lost Suzanne. That was careless."

Embarrassed look by me to Mark. "I think she got put off a little by our squabbling."

"With the greatest respect it's not all about you. Much more likely it's her love for Janet that drew her away. The good news is that I know exactly where she is, the bad news is that you've wasted three days while you fannyed about so you might as well stick around another couple of hours and enjoy the show."

"So where is she?"

"I've given Mark an address. There may be some issues of confidentiality so I've asked him to be discreet. She might not even have used her real name. But that's the least of your problems."

"So what's the greatest of our problems?"

"The first is that I need a spoon of honey and maybe some lemon juice. I'm on in 10 and I need to oil the tubes," she said pointing at her throat. "Particularly now I know I have so many fans in the audience," she added, giving me her lovely smile again.

"And the second greatest problem after we've sorted the diva's retainer?"

"I think Suzanne may be in danger."

"Then we should go straightaway."

"No point. For a start it's at the other end of the country so a few hours either way are not going to make much difference. Secondly it's not that kind of danger. It's not the immediate threat of violence.

Although she may have that as well. But she can generally handle herself in those circumstances better than you might think – better than the rest of us anyway, with the honourable exception of Mark here. No, it's a generalised insidious threat that's been creeping up on her and the same reason we wanted Janet to get out. I think Janet's losing her mind and it was beginning to affect Suzanne too."

"What makes you say that and why is everyone so protective of Janet anyway?" I asked.

"That reminds me," I said, taking the journal from out of a carrier bag, "have you seen this?"

Phe opened it and glanced at a couple of pages.

"No. I'm sorry John, I'm due on in a few minutes and I really do need the time to go through a few preparations. Not the least of which is get the setlist order to the guys as I want to make a couple of changes."

"But is this material you wrote for her?"

"No. Looks like that's straight out of Janet's head."

So we left her to it. We did stay for the concert or most of it anyway. I tried to talk to Mark but he was being a bit uncommunicative. I think he was blaming himself a bit for letting Suzanne out of his sight or maybe it was Janet. Either way he was restless and anxious to get off towards the end when they'd gone off stage but were doubtless going to come back on for an encore. I had really enjoyed it. I hadn't realised how talented Phe was.

"Shouldn't we stay and talk to Phe some more afterwards?" I asked him as he was putting his jacket on.

"No, she's told us all she's going to tell us."

"But that's virtually nothing."

"You clearly weren't listening."

"I was but we barely had a sentence from her."

"I mean to the music."

"I really enjoyed the music. I didn't think you did."

"I couldn't give a toss about the music."

"I don't understand."

"I mean the stories in the music. That's the way Phe talks, the way she communicates. It always has been. She weaves myth and all kinds of advice into her music. She's a storyteller. You weren't listening to the lyrics were you?"

I looked at him quizzically. "I was admiring the playing. I thought she was great. They all were. So what did she say?"

"We need to go."

"But she wanted us to stay for the concert."

"Yes and in the concert she told us to go. Right now."

I followed him out.

"Do we really need to go at this time of night?"

"Probably not, but I'm keen to get going. We wasted a couple of days and it was a mistake that could cost us."

"You've had a beer. Are you sure you're alright to drive – particularly overnight?"

"I don't as a rule, but it was pretty weak and I reckon I'm still legal. I'll do a few hours and then pull over. If you don't want to take over until morning that's fine. I think we need to get out of the hotel."

We picked up our luggage and checked out. By that time Mark had a couple of coffees and was feeling perky. I just wanted to sleep.

"So where are we going? I guess I ought to know in case I do feel like taking over."

"Some hospice. All you need to know is Aberdeen."

"Aberdeen? Brilliant."

This was going to be a long journey. We'd be lucky to get the other side of Birmingham before stopping. "Have you thought of taking the train, or flying?"

"We need the flexibility," Mark replied enigmatically, "although I told the hire company we'd probably be doing less than a hundred miles."

"I haven't read the contract but I'd bet we'll end paying more than if we'd bought a new car!"

"That might be an exaggeration but... let's just get off, shall we?"

Chapter Sixteen

Suzanne was ushered into an anonymous three storey tenement building. The stone façade was dark and brooding but the light inside was warm and welcoming. A short stocky lady with a rugged but beaming face was hurrying around a compact kitchen from which welcoming smells and heat were spilling over into a lounge stuffed with old patterned furniture, fussy wallpaper and floor lamps standing in each corner with thick shades and tassels.

I realised Doug had already turned to go. He caught my anxious glance but Irene came and held me by the elbow. She muttered something but I hadn't quite tuned in to the accent yet. But I understood the body language: she was inviting me to sit and be fussed over. "I have to go," Doug rather unnecessarily added. I couldn't ask him if he would return and he wouldn't have said because he was already gone.

I was tired from the journey and happy to accept the hot broth of indeterminate vegetable or meaty goodness. The furniture might have looked hideous but it was very comfortable and you could sink into it. I was surprised that you could spend so long sitting down not doing much on a journey and feel so drained and tired by it. It was warm and my eyes fell asleep before I did.

Did she drug me? I neither knew nor cared but was happy to escape into a safer place where I met Janet. I couldn't get her to answer any questions but she seemed happy enough. I walked along a line of paving stones with white flowered herbaceous plants lining a narrow courtyard. The building was a low single storey stone one, that couldn't have been any more than one room deep, but with multiple doors every twenty metres or so. In the centre there was a small capped tower with a large bronze bell. Underneath this there was some inscription on a stone plaque, but I didn't read what was on it. I just opened the dark red door and almost walked straight into Janet. I sat down opposite her, close enough to hold her hands. We smiled but didn't speak. That seemed to last forever. For Janet that was enough.

Then, in a flood, I was asking her so many questions without giving her time to answer. Or I ran out of time before she could answer. Either way I awoke slightly stiff in the legs and the neck where my head had slumped unsupported. I wasn't alarmed to find myself back in the armchair from my reverie.

I could hear Irene gently humming to herself in the kitchen. I realised my bag had gone. I tried to remember what was in it that would incriminate me. Bank cards and driving licence? No they were still in a purse on me. In any case I had used my real name in the end although not given my real or any fixed address. I guess there would probably be something that might give me away. "Oh what the hell, I won't be able to keep this pretence up for much longer anyway."

I thought that or did I say it out loud?

Irene stopped humming and put her head round the door. She said something but I couldn't make it out again. So she repeated it, more slowly this time as if talking to a child. I understood. She was just asking me how I was. I told her I felt better but dozy and thirsty. She promised tea and was gone.

After what seemed less than sixty seconds she came in with a tray including tea, sugar and biscuits. The sugar and biscuits were unnecessary although I wondered if I should express interest in the soggy custard creams out of politeness. But the tea was great. Not too hot. She had brought a pot, refilled my cup and sat down without saying anything. I told her about my dream. Perhaps I shouldn't but I didn't see any reason why not and was just making conversation with her to explain why I was feeling a bit dozy. I didn't mention Janet by name but I did describe the building.

She thought for a while before answering. "That's our hospice."

"But I don't think I've ever been there. I've only been to the office in town. I didn't even know if it really existed as a place or was something else."

"You have", and she lowered her voice and leaned forward to me conspiratorially as if others might be listening, "the persistence of memory."

"But how could I remember something that as far as I know may not exist?"

"How? Easy. Have you never held a stick in a fire a bit longer than you should?"

I didn't have the faintest idea where she was going with this.

"You pull it out and the end is still glowing brightly like the embers of the fire? Perhaps you twirled it around for your friend to admire. Perhaps you drew circles in the air. Your friend could see the moving stick but they could also briefly see the circle of light in the air where the stick had been."

I still didn't understand what she meant, or why it had any relevance to knowing a place I had never been to. But I could see that circle of bright orange fire late at night in a field behind our house where I suspected my sister had stolen and eaten all the bonfire toffees and which I knew my mother had bought earlier that week.

"I've taken your things upstairs. Do you want to see your room?"

I did, although I was reluctant to leave the armchair. I wanted to go back to sleep there and re-enter the same dream. But perhaps bed would be the best place to do that.

The room was small but serviceable. There was a bathroom on the top landing. The room overlooked the street. We were slightly out of town but it was still busy with people and traffic and I imagined it would be like that most of the day and night. The bed had an iron frame with no headboard. It reminded me of Victorian hospital beds. There was a wooden dresser with a large (too large) mirror. I realised what a fright I looked, hair clumped and alternately dry and greasy, blouse stained with soup. No, not soup. Oh my God, it's stale, dry, stiffened vomit! Even my stockings were torn and riding up from the heel.

Irene, who had been waiting patiently by the door for any questions, sensed my sudden self-consciousness and started to withdraw. I asked if there were any other guests. She beamed at me and adopted the speaking to a child voice again. No guests. Just you and I. You'll be quite safe. Then a little chuckle. "Just give us a holler or stamp your feet on the ceiling if you want anything."

I didn't want anything. Just to get these wretched clothes off, have a wash and sleep. Preferably now a deep dreamless sleep. Janet could wait. Even though it couldn't have been any more than mid-evening, once washed, I was in bed and fast asleep within minutes.

Hugh was now tootling up the A90 from Dundee. It was a bright cold morning. Nice for a drive. The road was quiet – just a few cars and one black van that overtook far too close and nearly took his wing mirror off. Hugh instinctively veered slightly towards the verge as it passed.

He was thinking about Janet. Thinking about the first time that they met. It was at university at an open lecture about behavioural change for wellbeing. As usual Hugh stumbled in late and was struggling to find a seat (it turned out to be one of the better attended sessions). A lady with long brown hair spotted him and gestured to an adjacent seat which she had occupied with a coat and bag and now removed. Hugh wasn't used to such courtesy (not on his Psychology course) and took this as a good sign.

They were there for very different reasons. Hugh was genuinely interested in both the subject matter and the visiting lecturer (who he'd seen as the author of a couple of books in the university bookshop). Janet was not. She was just killing time between seminars and it was raining outside.

She had a vague interest in finding out what 'wellbeing' was as it was not a term she had come across before. But on balance she just thought she could catch up with some reading for the next class. Janet was taking some mysteriously structured and bundled Computer Technology course that during this year's programme included topics on maths and games design. She had an essay and seminar to prepare for about recursive loops and algorithms in software programming. Little wonder, then, that she found herself distracted.

There was some sort of technical problem with the projector and the lecturer stopped after about seven minutes whilst the support staff were scurrying about the stage reaching under the furniture and lifting floor panels to check connections. Hugh found himself using the opportunity to run off at the mouth to the lady that had invited him to sit. He was describing the fact that he was putting his coat under the chair, stating the obvious about the weather and then asked Janet, as she had been invited to introduce herself, a direct question.

Janet looked at him properly for the first time. He asked her how long she'd been having trouble with dreams.

Janet just looked at him, trying to take in this seismic shift in a seemingly inane conversation to one she wasn't expecting to have. From niff naff and trivia to intimate and personal in a heartbeat.

There was an awkward pause on her part.

She was thinking about it and realised she had always had very vivid dreams and sometimes they would be recurring dreams that were the kind of nightmares that would cause her to wake up in a sweaty panic. The worst ones were where she would think she had woken up and then find that she hadn't. But lately it had been okay. She had got into the habit of doing her university work and essays through the night – particularly when she had an urgent deadline. Consequently she would wake late, straight from deep unconsciousness, get up quickly and be straight out to catch the campus bus without any intervening thoughts or dreams... or toast.

She saw Hugh looking at her writing pad.

She looked down to see if her occasional doodles in there revealed a tortured soul but there was nothing on the page she had open at the moment.

"How did you know?" she asked.

Hugh smiled, "Tell me about them."

"But I don't know you."

"Then I'm the perfect person to tell. I won't judge and I can't tell your friends any embarrassing secrets."

Almost against her will she started telling him some of the recurring themes she had. Not the most dangerous, private stuff perhaps but some of the environments and atmospheres. Hidden rooms and cupboards, spiral staircases, old institutional buildings with puddles in the corridor. Hugh asked her what she was afraid of, what was chasing her. It varies, she said, sometimes it's someone she knows but they are strangely changed and there's something wrong with them. More often the person or thing is not seen. She just knows he/she/it's there and he/she/it's going to kill her. She was about to give an example when the lecturer cleared her throat, tested her mike, 123, and launched back into what turned out to be a fairly vacuous and superficial homily to the psychological benefits of salsa dancing (with demonstrations and… heaven help us… she requested audience participation with some really tinny, trebly, backing music from an overdriven but underpowered Walkman).

Afterwards Janet asked Hugh again, "but how did you know?"

"It's a home banker, statistically," was all he said and he headed off clutching his books and hoping to get one signed.

Janet saw him again, waiting outside the science block a few weeks later and she told him her full name this time, what year she was in, what she was studying and suggested they go for a drink. She wasn't a drinker. But she was a talker and Hugh was a good listener.

A black van was approaching the outskirts of Aberdeen at high speed. They had to brake and swerve to avoid two motorbikes that were overtaking a small car around a bend. They flashed and sounded their horn. The bikers would have shaken their fists or made some other hand gesture had they not been too busy using both hands to stay alive and upright. They felt the instinctive clinch between their thighs and adjusted their balance to swerve around the two vehicles. Of course the first one, who had a clear view of the road, found it easy but the one following, trusting the judgement of the lead bike, overcompensated and skidded on the side of the road, kicking up gravel and had trouble stopping his back wheel weaving from side to side like a fish through a fast current. It took him a bit longer to regain control, open the throttle and speed away to join his companion.

Inside the van were three men. It was one of those vans that was wide enough to have three front seats. There was a solid barrier behind the cabin seats with a small reinforced viewing panel with a sliding hatch. In the back were separate compartments each secured by lockable doors. This was a different design to the van that Mark had driven away from and that Suzanne had hidden under a forgotten railway bridge. It was bigger for a start, with a square back and not really designed to be driven at speed.

"Bloody idiots," the big thickset driver Ken was shouting. Little Canary, the small blond man in the centre, said nothing. He was used to saying nothing. Perhaps he got his nickname after saying too much. Ben, the new boy, was nursing a bruised lip where Suzanne had smacked him. "Do they drive on the other side of the road in Scotland?" he asked. "I wouldn't mind that," responded Ken, "but not on both sides of the road at the same time."

Ben was still excited about being a part of his new gang. His day job was pretty boring and, although he was slowly building himself a reputation as the 'go to' man in data analysis and ad hoc reporting. But it wasn't resulting in any increased salary, bonuses or promotion prospects. His boss, on the other hand, was getting a bonus, freebie trips abroad for conferences, special mentions in company communications and she knew NOTHING, she understood NOTHING, she did NOTHING. Ben suspected that her good reputation was just built on his work which she would present in executive meetings as her own research.

Ken, despite his intimidating physique, was a friendly face on reception. He and Ben had struck up a friendship over the traditional male bonding territory of football, cars and even the weather. It turned out they supported the same football team. What were the chances of that? A local team with hundreds of thousands of followers.

But Ken's real passion was restoring old vehicles. In particular, antique fire engines, ambulances, army trucks and the like. Ben didn't have the money or the time for any non-essential vehicles but he did drive an old beat up Alfa Romeo which had attracted Ken's interest. Part of Ken's duties were to organise parking. More than once Ben had arrived late blaming the car and had to ask Ken to find him an improvised double-parking space in the car park. But when Ben was working late one wet and blustery night and couldn't start the car, and was beginning to panic, Ken came over to see if he could help. A bit of tarpaulin, some metal scraping and cleaning, a bit of Vaseline on the battery connections, plus a handheld hairdryer on the spark plugs seemed to do the trick.

Ken made some cryptic remarks about joining a club which Ben assumed staged some sort of specialist car rally or racing event. Ben agreed to attend the following weekend although, to be honest, he wasn't really paying attention. He was just keeping Ken sweet so he would fix the car so that he could go. Meanwhile he was happy to say yes. Anything to please his new best friend and get out of the rain.

Ben turned up at the map grid reference Ken had given him. It was at the appointed time and place (Ben double checked) but there was no-one there. There was a field, a small wood, an unspeakably pot holed track and not much else.

He was not prepared to wait around for long.

There are better things to do with your weekend than this, surely.

He was about to write it off when the Little Canary stepped out from behind a tree. Ben didn't know how long he had been there but presumably all the time.

"How do?" he chirped.

"Sorry I was told to meet someone here."

"Yes that's me."

"Oh okay… I'm Ben. Pleased to meet you."

"I'm Little Canary."

"Really? Do people have game names in this club?"

"That's what they call me."

Silence.

Luckily they both turned to see Ken making his way carefully up the track from some distance in an old prison van. He was swinging the vehicle extremely slowly from one side of the track to the other to avoid the deep ruts and puddles.

It was the same van in which they were now hurtling towards Aberdeen. Hurtling as much as the van would allow anyway. Ken had taken the limiter off it but it wasn't really designed for long journeys at speed.

In any case they were now getting closer to Aberdeen, seeing more houses and slower traffic. On the dashboard was a Sat Nav system with a subtle difference. They were getting closer and they could see that the target destination moved very slightly and very subtly now and then depending on the time lag.

This was because the target destination was not a place – it was a person.

Chapter Seventeen

I asked Irene where the hospice was. She said it was close enough to walk to. She gave me some directions.

I memorised the turns, left and right, but I'm afraid the street names meant nothing to me and didn't stick in my mind. I had a rough idea which way to start and, if I was right in what I thought I'd seen, or imagined I'd seen, then surely I should be able to recognise the building. If I didn't find it, well so what? I could try again, with better information. I just needed to be out and walking. It didn't really matter where.

Irene was happy for me to wander about. I wasn't a prisoner although she did warn me to be back by teatime. I still wasn't sure what the parameters of my care were meant to be. It seemed as if I should be proving continually that I needed her care, or be working to earn my stay in some way. I asked Irene if there was anything I could do for her. Shopping or housework I supposed. Irene told me brutally that 'my job was to sort my life out'. Put like that, trying to find Janet and find some answers seemed the right job to do for now and I felt slightly less bad about taking someone's place who undoubtedly needed it much more than me.

I was a mess of a kind I suppose. I had lost focus in my life or perhaps become too focussed on one thing and one person. And yet I couldn't help feel that Janet was worth it. That she needed help, she needed the kindness of strangers and the reassurance of friends. I would find her. My stay at Irene's would be brief, I promised myself, and then I'd move on with or without Janet.

Irene hovered around as I left. I half expected her to hand me a pack of sandwiches folded neatly into a square of greaseproof paper, or to check I had my scarf or a vest on.

There was something she wasn't saying but I didn't know whether it was better left unsaid or not.

So with a cheery, "I'll be back soon", and trying not to look back to see if the lace curtains were opened behind me, or even if there were any lace curtains, I managed to close the front door behind me (at the second attempt) and set off right... or was it left. I wanted to walk and if it meant going around the block vigorously to get back on the right road then that's what I would do. I walked off briskly and confidently as if I knew where I was going.

I was told to walk parallel to a cobbled street. The ground was rising so I knew it was probably the right way as Irene had said 'up' and I could see it through the occasional gap in the tenements. I turned right under a small bridge which took me to a walk by a disused section of canal which was lined with mature chestnut, sycamore and lime trees. It was a pleasant walk even though the wind was sharp and cold in my face and I had to keep my eyes on the ground rather than the view in order to avoid the dog crap. I then came across what looked like a modern housing estate with endless rows of clean pale houses and flats, very tasteful but a bit blank and anonymous. I went straight through this, trying not to look like a stranger when passed by groups of youths and young mothers as if adopting a casual nonchalance would change my appearance. They looked at me like I was some kind of alien being unencumbered, as I was, by gaggles of toddlers, a pushchair or at least a dog.

I headed for a tower at the end of one of the avenues which looked like it belonged to an older industrial building. I tried to read the faded painted sign on the wall. There were a couple of short names I couldn't make out and a proud boast of being the finest paper mill on the Dee or was it the Don. I couldn't make that out either, but whichever river it was I couldn't get any further this way as the canal was connected to the river at this point by a locked gate and weir. Beyond this was a busy A road that wasn't really designed to be crossed on foot. I had to wait for the traffic to thin, straddle the barrier and then run across. I don't recommend this to casual wayfarers but I couldn't see any other way of getting to the other side and I could have walked for miles in either direction.

Just on the other side of this, as I regained my breath, was a really narrow lane that ran in parallel to the big road. It was not more than a footpath and was enclosed by hedges. Perhaps this was the old road before the new one was built. I followed it up the slope. Irene had kept saying "up". Of course anywhere from the river level was bound to be up, or along, but I was sure I was still going in the right direction. It just seemed a lot further than Irene had described it. I think I must have needed to find this old road earlier and not go around the housing estate and across the new A road. That diversion had taken me in an unnecessary loop but it was where the modern road builders were funnelling all the traffic now. Perhaps Irene was unaware of the new housing development which looked like it had been thrown up in a panic to meet government targets and then promptly abandoned to market forces to provide, or not provide, any necessary local amenities and services.

This road curved sharply to the right and here there were a set of older stone buildings. I recognised the colour of the stone from my dream. The buildings were low and had turned their backs to the new road.

I tried to find a way around to the front. Maybe there was a courtyard on the other side, judging by the square of rooflines heading off at right angles to the main terrace.

And where was the bell tower that I had seen?

I walked along the back of the row expecting to see into small bedrooms and have to apologise, for prying, to anyone looking out towards the path or lane which now ran right past their windows.

I did see one person – they had a drink in their hand and quickly looked away from me, as if talking to someone else in the room that I couldn't see.

At the end of the row it opened up into a car park. There was a fence and, behind some large wheely bins, there was a pub sign. I walked around the front expecting to see the courtyard I'd envisioned but instead there was just a single low, modern, red brick, double porch on the front of another older stone building – presumably it was the entrance to the pub. Damn. This wasn't the right building. And I had been so sure.

Why had I expected to find a building that I'd only seen in a dream, in a city I didn't know, following only half-understood directions?

Then I began to think about the trance-like state that I had entered into when walking, running or travelling lately.

This time I had been completely clear headed throughout the walk. I had been thinking, not dreaming.

Did I need to think less clearly?

No, that was nonsense. I needed my wits about me when, or if, I find Janet. I want this to be real.

I looked up and saw someone watching me through the glass double-door.

I felt self-conscious with this pub customer or more likely, at this time of day, an idle member of bar staff or manager who was watching me so intently, even though I must have been a good thirty feet away across the car park. But I wasn't tempted to go in, use the loo or buy a drink and ask directions. Why should I? They could go to hell.

To one side there were a set of trees – not exactly a woodland, just a visual barrier that I couldn't see what was beyond. There was a small path of mud and broken bramble which people had obviously used as a sort of custom and practice footpath or shortcut to and from the pub.

Shortcut from where?

I still couldn't see anything through the trees. I looked back and that person with the pinned-up hair, who obviously had nothing better to do, was still looking at me as if I had just landed from Mars.

Out of instinct I just stepped towards and then into the wood to get out of sight.

After taking only one or two steps in, I could see another low-lying building slightly further down the brow of the hill. It was made of the same stone and in the same style as the pub. Perhaps they had both been part of some bigger estate when they were built a couple of hundred years ago. So people from this building obviously used the path as a shortcut to and from the pub rather than going around by road. Made sense. Particularly if they wanted a wee dram or five.

I was probably straying onto private property but there weren't any signs to deter me. When I got to the corner of the building I looked up and down for some sort of indication as to what sort of place this was. It was too big for a private house. It looked like an old stable block and there, in the centre, was a blue domed tower with a dark, bronzed, bell above a white and blue faced clock. Although the tower was twice the height of the surrounding single storey building you couldn't see it until you turned into the surrounding courtyard. Unless, of course, you approached from the lower road in the opposite direction up a wide drive, lined with pollarded lime trees, and clearly designed in the days of horse drawn carriage rather than with any modern street furniture and horseless carriage in mind. Was there a plaque on the wall? Yes I think so but I was too far away to be able to read it. I couldn't see anyone around although there was a small white van parked to one side with ladders on the roof rack. There were no other vehicles in sight.

I approached gingerly as if I was a prospective burglar, walking slowly and constantly checking to left and right. I checked my handbag for the gun as some sort of reassurance. It wasn't there. Irene must have confiscated it. I don't know why I hadn't noticed the difference in weight but to be honest it was a relief. I didn't want the responsibility of having to threaten somebody with it let alone use it. And anyway I was just here to see Janet wasn't I?

Which was the right door? There were so many and all of them were identical. Now I was closer I could see they had numbers and large brass knockers. Some had stone pots and troughs outside full to the brim with bright cheery annual flowers. I didn't remember those from my dream. Perhaps I just hadn't noticed them.

I tried to think back again to that moment but couldn't remember which door. It seemed so vivid and yet within minutes I'd forgotten almost everything that I said and did in the dream. I just remember

Janet was so calm and reassuring. Which is odd because that is exactly the feeling I was hoping to bring to her as I felt she was probably in more need of it than me.

I still couldn't see any signs but I was pretty sure now that this was the hospice. So, out of desperation, I tried to unthink my conscious mind and just head for a door and knock.

Nothing.

I knocked again. Louder and more insistent this time.

Nothing, although I thought I could hear a slight scraping like the dragging of heavy furniture on a stone floor.

I hadn't come all this way just to be ignored so I knocked again.

At last an answer.

Someone opened a door but it was the next one down to the one I'd been knocking on.

A lady with grey hair, large white earrings and a pearl necklace, looked at me sideways and said, "she's not there."

"Oh," I said, "do you know when she will be back?"

"She won't be back. There'll be somebody else in next week."

"What happened to her? Did she go away? Do you know where?"

"She died."

"What?" I could feel the wind knocked right out of me and felt weak at the knees.

The lady must have noticed my distress and said, "Oh I'm sorry dear. Didn't you know? Were you close?"

"Yes…" I gasped, "I loved her."

"Oh my dear, were you her daughter?"

"What?"

"Were you related?"

"No."

"Oh, only I think she said she had a daughter somewhere abroad but had lost touch with her. I think the authorities tried to trace her so the family had time to travel for the funeral, but I don't think they could find her. It was very quiet. Bit of a shame, don't you think?"

She looked at me accusingly but then you could almost see the penny dropping for both of us as the old lady tried to recalibrate. "I think you'd be a bit young for her daughter, my dear. I expect she would be in her forties or even fifties by now. You never know, as people seem to have children really early these days… so you could be her granddaughter I suppose."

"No, I'm really sorry. I must have made a mistake. I was looking for someone called Janet."

"Oh. Janet you say? Three doors down. Number 2," she mumbled and she turned away and slammed the door as if annoyed to have wasted her time even though I was pretty sure I hadn't disturbed anything more than a loud radio show and maybe a session with a donated jigsaw with pieces missing.

So much for the psychic powers and trusting your instinct, I thought, as I set off down the line.

I was now in front of the right door.

Deep breath.

What was I going to say? I didn't know but if I hesitated now I'd never knock, so I did.

There was a little round peephole in the door with a brass cover on the inside. It flickered open and I could see a slightly distorted fish eye which flashed through the other side of it.

There was a pause and then some rattling of a door chain. The door opened a crack and I could see an eighth of Janet's face.

"It's me," I said.

"Yes," she said. "I worked that out. Are you on your own?"

"Of course," I said, involuntarily looking round as if to find out myself whether I was alone and to prove to her I was telling the truth.

She closed the door and for a moment I thought that was it. There was more rattling of the door chain or multiple chains and then she opened the door wide.

I stepped in and was surprised how monk-like and small the room was. Just an armchair and a fairly uncomfortable two-seater settee. No TV. There was a sideboard and that was it. You could see straight out of the back window and would be able cross the room in three steps. To each side there was an open door. One was a small kitchenette and through the other I think I could see a single wire framed bed. Presumably there was a toilet and sink off this room somewhere although I couldn't imagine how it would all fit in the space. Perhaps it wrapped around the next door flat in an L-shape as the bedroom seemed too close to the next front door in the row.

I moved to hug her but she shifted her weight slightly sideways, shrugging, and then sat down.

"What's wrong?"

"You're here."

"Look, I can understand why you felt you needed to get away, to get clear away from people you knew and thought you could trust, but anything we did to protect you was out of love, not anything else. Frankly we didn't know what to do."

"Yes," Janet mumbled.

"Has it helped?"

She didn't answer. Instead she asked, "Why are you here?"

"Because I felt this wouldn't get resolved unless we took some action. I lost faith in the boys knowing what they were doing."

"Well you're not wrong there."

"I don't think they had the patience to listen to our story the way we originally envisaged it. They just wanted to leap straight into action and run around. They thought I was a damsel in distress and it took them a while to realise it was really all about you."

"I'm not sure that's true. You wanted to tell our story. I never did."

"Didn't you?"

"No."

"Why not?"

Again Janet wouldn't answer. She flicked her hair off her forehead away from her left eye. It had grown longer since I'd last seen her and could really do with the attention of a hairdresser.

"You're looking well," I said. She was. There was certainly more colour in her cheeks and she had put on a bit of weight (I've never been a fan of people being too skinny except when it comes to myself of course.)

Janet continued staring into the middle distance. Why was this so awkward? I wished now I'd written a list of questions and could conduct this more like an interview. I couldn't help feeling that time was running short. Now was the time for honesty and openness if we were to rescue this relationship. Ah well, in for a penny...

"What about us?" I asked. "What about the future... for us? We used to think we could conquer the world – just the two of us, together."

"You're right about one thing Suzanne. You can only know what the future will be, can be, should be, if you study your own past more carefully and understand it."

"So?"

"You're a thief," she said, "you stole my heart at a party but that's not all you stole."

"I did go through a brief phase of stealing things when I was a teenager. We talked about that. It was nothing, although I did include it in my little confessional because you mentioned it before and it seemed to bother you."

"It was something that mattered to me. In any case I was really talking about later. It had nothing to do with your totally unnecessary self-centred psycho-babble, and your absurd blaming of your parents for every wrong decision you've ever made in your life. You were just seeking sympathy, or maybe absolution, from your new friends if they knew how tough life has been for you... not!"

"I don't understand."

"Do I have to spell it out for you?"

"I wish you would."

"When we met I was just starting my work at Harman and it was all laboratory based. I didn't bring my work home. At least not until much later. But somehow just as I was beginning to make progress it began to *infect* you. I still don't understand how. My job was software. There was a biotech unit but I wasn't on that side of the corridor. Just code. That was me. Just numbers. Just puzzles and algorithms. Yet somehow you got infected by it, like a virus. You had no symptoms but you were a born carrier and everything then changed between us. I became sick and you were completely oblivious to it all. So we had to change the plan although, in truth, I was just improvising. There was no plan."

"What plan are you talking about? Or not talking about? You mean the plan for us?"

Janet was silent once more and wouldn't hold my gaze. She seemed to be looking around for something. Was she planning right now or improvising? I used to joke that I could always tell what she was thinking, that she was so transparent, but I realised I no longer could. Maybe I never could and was only just now realising it.

I followed her glance through the window. There was a grass bank taking up most of the view. I thought there was virtually nothing there to see but I noticed a small glimpse back to the main drive on one side; perhaps Janet had a better view of it from her side of the room. There may have been something dark moving there but, if so, it was gone now.

This certainly wasn't going according to my plan. I'd expected Janet to greet me like a long-lost lover or at least a sister. She was curiously cold. As blank and anonymous as this flat. I looked around it again.

There were no photos, no newspapers, no phones or gadgets, no coats, shoes or clothes I recognised. It was like a hotel room only with no welcoming comforts. No chocolates on the pillow. Not even a mini kettle nestled amongst sachets of coffee and tea. It was more like what I imagined a motel to be like - suitable as a brief stopover cell in a human garage, for sleeping not for living.

"What plan?" I asked again.

"Not the whole plan but a plan for you."

"You're creeping me out Janet. This is not like you."

"You don't know me. You don't own me. None of you own me."

The door burst open and I was grabbed from behind. Whoever it was had their arms tightly around my chest and arms straight away. I tried to turn but couldn't. Someone in black passed me and grabbed Janet. The two men, I think they were men, put a hood over my head but I could still see their black boots. There must have been three or four of them. People that is, not feet. I could hear Janet trying to say something. Strangely I couldn't cry out. It was like a dream where you think you are screaming but nothing is coming out, or maybe it was and I couldn't hear it. I was now being bound around the wrists. A disgusting handkerchief which smelled awful was put in my mouth and the hood was tightened around my chin. I tried to kick my legs, which were still free, and I got one of them pretty hard on the shin. They cried out and swore at me. Then there was a sharp pain in my arm and I was being dragged backwards by my head and shoulders. Good, I thought, they've left my legs free. I'll take another swing at them.

But I was beginning to feel so tired and to lose focus. I could feel the colder air of outside and the sound of metal banging. But rather than being revived and refreshed by it I got the sensation of it all drifting away. I felt the impact of being pulled into a room or something up a step and a door closing as I collapsed.

Chapter Eighteen

Hugh was too late. He'd found Doug at the hospice and was describing Suzanne to him. Doug knew who he was talking about straightaway but he was not giving anything an inch as confidentiality was paramount in his thinking.

"Her life may be in danger", Hugh was pleading.

"All of our lives are in danger", Doug said. "People who come here are often in danger of one thing or another, that's why they come."

Hugh explained that Suzanne's motive was to find someone called Janet. For the first time, Hugh observed, there was a flicker of some reaction from Doug. An involuntary, and no doubt subconscious, flick around his right eye.

So it seems Suzanne didn't level with the hospice. As well as using a false name, she had given no indication that her objective was trying to find someone else.

As Hugh described Janet's physical appearance, what was it Hugh could read on Doug's face? Betrayal? The thought of being used? Twice? He obviously cared for Janet or was it Suzanne or maybe he just cared for all his charges and was now having to reassess these people he'd trusted.

But he still wasn't giving anything away.

It was an urgent phone call, put through by the secretary, that broke the stalemate of Hugh's circular questions and fruitless entreaties. Irene insisted on speaking to Doug straight away and he hadn't time to ask Hugh to leave before answering. Although it was just a telephone conversation Irene was shouting on the other end and Hugh could hear clearly enough. She was mortified and apologetic but Suzanne, or whatever her name was, was missing. And there was more. She had confiscated a gun and not told anybody until now. She thought she was doing the right thing in case of potential suicide or worse. It hadn't crossed her mind Suzanne might be in danger from somebody else but now the idea had occurred to her it also made her panic. She cursed herself for not calling Doug earlier when she was told there had been a serious incident at the accommodation block. Police were on site. They were called because two women were seen being bundled into a black van and driven off at high speed by a grey-haired neighbour... well at the speed of 20 miles an hour over the speed bumps but, admittedly, with a great deal of unnecessary revving.

Doug was clearly shaken by this news, and not a little angry. Never, in all his time at the hospice etc... But primarily his concern was for Irene and to absolve her of all blame, guilt and worry. You can only do so much for people etc... He would take responsibility. He would sort it out.

But he still wouldn't speak directly to Hugh about it. Hugh was beginning to admire this taciturn priest although he was pretty sure that he wasn't going to sort anything out except make Irene feel better and protect the important work of the centre for the sake of other waifs and strays. Hugh's casual acquaintance with the cloth had led him to suppose the clergy was populated by middle class idiots who were at best hypocrites and at worst snake oil salesmen and women. But Doug's ministry was something tougher and it didn't totally surprise Hugh when the police turned up at the office less than five minutes later and asked him to accompany them to the local station but not Doug who they obviously knew and treated as a trusted friend.

He didn't bother to ask the police whether his attendance was meant to be voluntary or whether he was being arrested under caution for some offence.

Hugh was questioned and cross-examined by a couple of detectives after being booked in by a stone-faced sergeant who insisted the PC check his pockets for drugs and sharp objects. Initially they treated him as a suspect and were checking everything he said and claimed by cross-referencing it on a call with the West Midlands police. Guilty until proved innocent seemed to be the approach. There were a lot of forms to fill in but eventually the Scottish Police Authority started treating him as a witness and, by the end, more as a victim (offering tea and sympathy).

As part of the process Hugh had been asked for contact names and numbers of relatives and friends. Apparently he hadn't been arrested. He didn't remember there being any choice when three burly peelers manhandled him out of the hospice, pushed his head in the back of a car and refused to talk to him on the short journey to the station. So when he made his call later to Mark it still felt like this was his obligatory single phone call and would be the last desperate contact he would have with the outside world for a while rather than to say he was free.

"Hi Mark, can you talk?"

"I'm driving but I'm with John – perhaps he can put you on speakerphone?"

"Hello Mark?"

"Mark?"

"That's better. You've got it. Hi Hugh, can you hear me?"

"Just about."

"Where are you?"

"Well that's it. I'm in a police station."

"Ah. I knew they'd get you eventually. Is it the kiddie porn collection or the drugs?"

"Listen Mark. This is serious. I'm in Aberdeen. I was trying to reach Suzanne. I think she's been taken."

"Oh. What are doing in the police station? Reporting it?"

"They think I had something to do with it. Now I guess they think you do too. There's worse. I think they've got Janet as well."

There was cursing and swearing on the other end. Hugh had to move the phone away from his ear. When he replaced it Mark was asking, "What do you expect us to do about it?"

"I don't know. I just thought you should know."

"It sounds like you had the same thought as us. As luck would have it we're not a million miles away and heading in your direction."

"I'm in Queen Street. Can you get here?"

"Don't you think it would be better for us to find the girls?"

"No, come here. There's some things I need to tell you and", he added in a hushed tone turning away from anyone in earshot, "I don't want to do it over the phone."

"I didn't catch that but we'll head to you. Won't be for about an hour."

The phone connection dropped without either pressing anything but both parties knew the conversation was over... for now.

As the Police had lost interest in Hugh he was politely asked to leave. He asked them if there was any news but was told that they couldn't say. Whether that was couldn't or wouldn't was impossible for Hugh to tell.

Hugh tried to call Mark again. It went straight to voicemail. Hugh didn't leave a message. He found a nearby coffee shop and tried again. Straight to voicemail so he left a message this time to meet in the coffee shop.

After a couple of coffees he wondered whether to go back to the hospice but was reluctant. Nonetheless he was getting the 'are you going to buy an Eccles cake?' sort of look from the staff in the coffee shop, despite the fact that it was half empty and they didn't really need the table.

Mark and John hadn't got Hugh's message about the coffee shop and headed for Queen Street. They found a car park and walked to the station past the coffee shop. Mark was looking ahead, trying to see signs for the police station, John was looking at his phone as was Hugh, sitting in the window. John was trying to get Google Maps the right way up. He'd plugged in the walk to the Police Station but found he was walking in the wrong direction – three times. Mark, in frustration, decided to use the dead reckoning of common sense and use his eyes. It was likely to be in a prominent position and sign posted. Queen Street. There it was on the left. A little way in and up on the right was a big grey building with a handy sign saying "Police". I wonder if that could possibly be it thought Mark smugly. He would have spoken to John but he was now 200 yards behind staring at his phone and walking straight past the turning. He'll catch me up, eventually, thought Mark.

He entered the building after trying to work out how the reception security for visitors was supposed to operate. He had to fill in some more paper forms and wait. Mark also made sure he opened his wallet in front of the civilian manning the door so that she could see his West Midlands police ID in there. Won't do any harm he thought despite how territorial the regional forces still are. He could also see John outside the building trying to work out how to get in, took pity on him and triggered the automatic door for him. They waited together in virtual silence with Mark resisting the temptation to tell John what he thought of his navigation skills.

Eventually a detective came out. She asked who John was. Mark said he was a friend. There was some sort of coded understanding between the two police officers, perhaps a gesture or a look, that led to the detective asking John if he could step outside a moment.

"Bloody masons," John muttered under his breath as he hit the exit button.

The exchange between Mark and the detective, Lorna, was brief and courteous but also slightly wary as they spoke in bullet points like a notebook report.

- Hugh had been released and wasn't under suspicion.
- They were aware of Mark's association with the West Midlands Police... and his ambiguous employment status.
- Mark confirmed that his presence was in no way official.

- He gave Lorna brief physical and character descriptions for Suzanne, Janet, Hugh and John (no mention of Pheona). She took notes.

- Lorna told Mark (against common practice) what information they had on the suspects: black van with partial but unreliably witnessed number plate, three men with different builds, casual clothes. No further sightings but checking CCTV for direction of travel.

- Lorna didn't tell Mark that, in the course of their investigations, they had recovered a lightweight pistol with a GPS tracking device on the base of the handle. It was currently with the techies for fingerprints and further analysis but they didn't think that it had been fired recently, there was no ammunition recovered and, although technically in working order, it was likely to be a hobby or antique collector's item.

- As a parting shot Mark told Lorna it might be worth checking the records of current and past security employees at Harman. Might be a waste of time, might not.

That was it. The conversation probably took no more than 5 minutes. Lorna insisted on checking Mark's mobile phone number by ringing it before letting him go, then turned sharply on her heels and back through the secure door into the core of the building. In responding to the phone Mark noticed a text message from John saying he'd heard from Hugh and was going back to a coffee shop round the corner.

Meanwhile Hugh had given up on both of them and was walking back to the hospice.

Chapter Nineteen

Suzanne was dreaming about war in Asia again although this time she was being moved from one camp to another. She hadn't seen any Japanese or Thai soldiers and wasn't sure how she knew it was a forced march but it was very hot again and uncomfortable. She heard a woman's voice shouting in the distance but she couldn't make out what she was saying. She didn't want to know. She knew that the best chance of survival lay in keeping her eyes down, not challenging the guards and not engaging with her fellow prisoners. She must have drifted off to sleep again.

When she woke again she realised that she was slumped on a floor in a dried pool of urine and her clothes were also stiff from dried sweat. She could make out some bars, which had created shadow stripes on her bare legs, and she ached all over.

She certainly felt as if she had been on a force marched through the jungle but the tiny cell that held her was mostly rigid plastic. There was a bench, which incorporated a chemical toilet, and very little else. It was closed on three sides but the bars where she was slumped revealed a narrow corridor and there must be a window to one side where natural light was coming in. There was also electric light recessed into the ceiling but this was switched off from somewhere outside the cell.

Should she call out? What would be the point? Just to announce that she was awake and not very happy?

She decided just to listen with her eyes shut and, if anyone came, she would pretend to still be asleep although she did permit herself the luxury of stretching and twisting her muscles and getting into a more comfortable position. Had she been more observant she would have noticed the video camera but as it happens her captors were too busy arguing to watch it anyway.

She could hear voices very faintly. Too faintly even to tell what sex they were. She could also hear birdsong and the complete absence of traffic or any industrial or road noise. Did she imagine hearing distant sheep? Little Bo Peep went back to sleep.

"Suzanne! Suzanne! Are you alright?"

This time she woke properly.

"Janet?"

"Are you alright? You've been asleep absolutely ages."

"I know. I think they must have given me something."

"Thank goodness you're alright."

I couldn't see Janet. But she was close. It must be the next-door cell. I tried to slip my arm through the end gap in the bars but could only get my arm out up to my elbow. Janet did the same and we touched fingers, interlocking and squeezing in reassurance.

Then the sound of a sliding door and she quickly pulled her hand away. Heavy footsteps and a metal tray appeared at the end of hairy tattooed arms. There was a hatch to one side of the cell with a horizontal slot underneath. As the tray emerged on my side of the bars I could see the face of a heavyset man in his late forties. He didn't speak. I didn't speak. He turned away and left as I heard the heavy door slide closed.

"Janet?" I mouthed almost silently, then whispered it again a little louder.

"Eat up. You'll need it."

Of course, it was food. Well at least that was something, although I couldn't imagine how they'd got any drink through the narrow horizontal slit. I opened the tray. There was a metal sachet of drink with a straw and some pretty unappetising cold, stiff, lumpy porridge.

"I'm not sure I need my strength that badly."

"Why? What have you got?"

"Same as you I suppose."

"No, I ate earlier. Bacon bap."

"You lucky so and so. I've got porridge."

"Oh good grief! I think that's someone's idea of a joke... doing porridge. Mind you, thinking about it, it's much better for you than what I had."

"The drug didn't knock you out so badly then? I still feel like I've gone a few rounds with a Sumo wrestler who then left me to sleep with my body twisted in on itself in some kind of knot."

"I guess not – no pun intended. Eat up."

"You sound like my mum."

"I mean it." Just then an engine started up. We must be in some sort of lorry or a portacabin on a lorry as the cell started to vibrate.

I didn't eat the porridge. Not because I don't like porridge but on principle. I would rather starve than accept anything from these people. But the drink, that was another matter. I was seriously dehydrated. In any case it was a sealed sachet. If they'd put extra knockout drops in anywhere it would surely be in the food.

I swore as I choked on some of the liquid when we drove over what felt like a series of tree roots, hollows and banks. We were now back on a regular road. I could tell because the vehicle was picking up speed and I could hear the whoosh of occasional passing traffic.

"Janet?" I called out. And again.

No response. Perhaps she couldn't hear me over the road noise.

I tried again.

Perhaps she'd fallen asleep. Maybe the drugs in her food had taken effect.

I tried to get some sense of direction from the Sun but I had no window and in any case it was an overcast grey day or maybe it was the next day but still too early for the sun to be any height or strength. I had no idea.

I wondered whether to count in order to get an impression of distance. I figured a rough speed and by that figured we were going about a mile a minute. Unfortunately I had no watch on so after counting for what I thought might be about 10 miles I got bored and gave up.

I felt around for my phone. Stupidly I thought it would be there. Of course it wasn't.

I called out for Janet.

No response, again, although I thought I heard her shuffle in her cell.

This was going to be a long day.

Chapter Twenty

Hugh was sitting with Doug when John and Mark (who had just found each other) caught up with him at the hospice. They were in the waiting room. It was the only room that was big enough to have four people sit down and talk.

Doug introduced himself to the two newcomers and then asked them to do the same. By that I mean that Doug gave a strangely full biography of where he was born, where he grew up, what jobs he'd done, what led him to the priesthood, the work of the centre and how it was funded. He said it was important in his line of work that you knew who people were, what made them tick and that they were brutally honest. Particularly, he said, under the current circumstances and he looked pointedly at Hugh. I had no idea what his problem was. He continued that, if we didn't mind, he'd like us to introduce ourselves fully and frankly. It felt like an interview to me, or some embarrassing business meeting icebreaker, but I tried to go along with it. Mark was fairly open about his past – both the good and the bad – with some things that I didn't know and that made my jaw drop.

Apparently Doug was from Glasgow. His family were from an industrial background. Not shipbuilding but some sort of specialist engineering. Both parents worked at the same factory. He said he didn't have much in common with them and took more after his uncle who got him interested in Biblical Studies. Mark and I exchanged looks, as if questioning who Doug's real father was, but fortunately Doug didn't notice our cheeky glance. The uncle worked as a clerk in a shipping office and used to take him, with some of the other kids who worked there, to a voluntary dockside creche run by a kindly old woman (at least she seemed old to them) called Irene Bell.

Privately I was thinking of all the nicknames the kids would have come up with for her (Tinkerbell, Clanger etc) but actually her name 'I ring bell', which was how Doug pronounced it, was good enough on its own.

Doug was very passionate about the work of the hospice. He explained that they didn't just look after the ill and the mentally and emotionally damaged casualties of an industry that could still be isolating and brutal. They also offered legal advice on wages, contractual issues, international disputes and practical help for thousands of ordinary employees. I guess I'd thought of them as a quasi-Catholic spiritual refuge for people trying to 'find themselves', in a Californian hippie sense, but realised they operated much more as a vital health, wealth and practical counselling service for people who just had no equivalent company function to look after their wellbeing (or at least that could be trusted and be independent enough to help them).

Now it was my turn. I was a little embarrassed to follow Doug's heartfelt history with my rather mundane and happy childhood and early career. I was born in the English Midlands (in Shropshire). My dad was a travelling insurance salesman (and my occasional days out with him were the nearest I got to any sense of adventure). My mother was 'just a housewife'. I could hear everybody cringe when I said this but how else could you put it. That was what she did. Of course she was doing an important job, and doing it with her customary sophistication and elan, but it was pointless to disguise the different standards of that time. If you'd have asked her what she was, she would have said that she was a housewife and, if pressed, was proud that her husband's earnings enabled her to concentrate on bringing up the children. I guess that little word 'just' in my description had betrayed my tacit complicity in disregarding it as a career choice.

What was there to say about my adult life? I left education. I didn't follow my peers from grammar school to university as I was impatient to start earning money. I did some junior admin roles, moved around, got promotion. The problem was that work defined me and defined my view of my family. This was not what was important to Doug or any of the others. Strange how spilling this little biography into the brutal light of day immediately gave me other people's perspective on myself. As I was thinking what to say next I suddenly realised that Suzanne was important. She gave my life meaning. I wasn't sure what that meaning was, but as I spoke about my pathetic sounding job at Harman, and I could see my audience's eyes glaze over, what became painfully obvious to me was that my involvement in whatever this was, here and now, was an attempt to finally find some meaning in my life. But, of course, I didn't say that, and my description of myself just sort of tailed off into a mumble and then silence.

Mark jumped in to save my embarrassment and described his services childhood, mostly in Germany but also in Gibraltar, Malta, unspecified African countries and in the States. His parents didn't get on too well. Both were in the services, often posted to different countries. When they were together they would often fight; his mother being the more aggressive of the two. Alcohol had a diametrically opposed affect on them. His father would just fall asleep whereas his mother would get, at first, overly sentimental and loving, then aggressive and engineer a fight. The combination of the two, when they drank together, was not good. Mark mostly followed his mother around but as he got older he got to spend more time with his father. He had a lot of time to himself than any child I knew and he had no sister or brother. This left him at the mercy of whatever local gangs of older children or teenagers were around. He learnt to look after himself physically but he was lonely and resentful. He developed the ability to socialise with people of all ages but, when offered any opportunity of genuine friendship, he would always shy away from it. He told himself this was to protect the other person, as inevitably he would be leaving for another country, but it was fundamentally to avoid him being open to any emotion.

He joined the Army more or less to give himself somewhere to live when he came of age. Training was a breeze. He'd been doing most of the physical exercises all his life and was able to concentrate on some of the technical learning. Mark was uncharacteristically vague about what units he joined and what his training actually was. I got the impression that he had joined some sort of unit gathering intelligence so I guess his vagueness and playing things down was a question of observing Official Secrets. But one thing he was quite specific about shocked me. He was sacked for killing a prisoner. Except they don't call it sacking in the Army. Dishonourable discharge or something like that. Apparently it wasn't during an interrogation or rendition of any kind. The prisoner just went crazy and started beating one of his captors to a pulp. Mark heard the commotion and stepped in, killing him with his bare hands. The guard had severe facial injuries where his nose and eye sockets had been pierced and pulped with a metal object. Mark was bitter about the fact that he had been trained to kill and then faced disgrace for the fact that his training automatically kicked in. He was told he should have simply restrained the prisoner. How do you restrain a homicidal person with a weapon on your own? You use extreme force. You have to. For Mark it was 'him or me'. But it turned out the prisoner was some big shot important guy and the politics of his detention were labyrinthine and complex. Certainly well above Mark's pay grade to be told anything. He just felt he was sacrificed in some sort of international deal that was everything to do with unspoken vested interests in global trade and nothing to do with individual behaviour or responsibility.

With typically obtuse governmental hypocrisy Mark found himself shunned by his army bosses and former colleagues but "looked after" by some anonymous benefactor who had intervened and arranged a cushy job in a specialist unit of the police. This ultimately made it feel more like a transfer than a humiliation although his new police bosses and colleagues persisted in giving him less than affectionate nicknames like 'Mr. Reject' and 'second hand Mark'. Those were the cleaner and less abusive names. This specialist police unit was mostly undercover and covert. Consequently Mark didn't have to see his colleagues very much or have to get along with them. The only time he would mix with them socially was if he had to go to a station to take part in an 'interrogation', sorry 'interview', of some suspect or witness. He liked his work but had started to drift and lose motivation as he would never be given a case to see through from start to end. They would just give him odds and sods. He also said he missed the camaraderie of an army unit. Where you would give your life for your buddies and know they would do the same. It was just you and your mates against the world, against the enemy, against the 'Ruperts' (army slang for officers). So he asked the police for a period of time off. A sort of sabbatical. Against expectations they agreed. In fact they seemed quite eager. That's when he had hooked up with one of the civvies he'd met leading some sport psychology courses for injured or traumatised ex-forces at a local leisure centre – a guy called Hugh – who suggested he take a job in security at Harman's to pay the rent. Over to you Hugh.

I interjected. "It's all very well going down Memory Lane but aren't we supposed to be rescuing somebody?"

Doug said, "I'm not sure about who's rescuing who but Hugh has a plan. Listen to him."

"Okay I'll spare you talking too much about myself" he said, looking in Mark's direction, "but I do need to tell you about Janet and Suzanne and why we've a bit more time than you think. Firstly Janet. I have a bit of a soft spot for Janet and I think that has prevented me from analysing her as objectively as I might. I knew her at University and we'd been close. Not as close as I would have liked but good friends, I think. She's changed and matured during the time she has been working at Harman and if I take that person, and ignore everything I knew about her from before, then I have realised that I would have come to a very different conclusion. I was fascinated by her journal because there were elements in it which were clearly experiential. She had been there and done some of those things but I think she had manipulated the timeline and location. I don't believe that everything took place in a single sequence. I think it took place in spurts and she put it together later. Some of it was virtual, some of it was physical, and that was a deliberate effort to blur the barriers between the two. I don't think she was ever as sick or as lost as she would have us believe, at least not until now."

"As for Suzanne I think there was some sort of transference that took place. Her intimacy with Janet somehow allowed her to share Janet's experience. I suspect that this was triggered at a deep emotional, psychological and empathetic level, not physically like a virus. I did consider the biological transference and it lead me down an interesting, complex, but ultimately futile speculation. What I've realised is that this operated, at least in their case, like an athletes' relay race in the Olympics track and field. At the moment Suzanne started to share some of these experiences as a complete "natural", without the aid of the research technology and chemicals, then Janet lost faith in what she was doing. It's a shame that it wasn't the opposite and I still haven't been able to work out why. You would have thought Janet would have been delighted and fascinated to see where Suzanne's experience might lead. Instead she became jealous and disconcerted by Suzanne. Janet's behaviour has been increasingly one of resentment and deceit; at least as far as this group is concerned. She withdrew into herself largely as a means of buying time to decide what to do and how to regain commercial advantage from it."

There was a bit of a pause while we tried to process this information but I found Hugh's explanations lacking. "That's all very well, Hugh, but I don't understand how it gets us any nearer to finding either of them. They are in physical danger, yes? I imagine their psychological and emotional wellbeing at the moment is directly related to that."

"What I'm trying to explain," said a clearly exasperated Hugh, "but I've only had chance to tell Doug so far, is that I've been following some fresh clues and assumptions which I think we can use to find both Janet and Suzanne. I wanted to tell you before you got to the Police but I didn't get the chance. Mark was supposed to infiltrate himself in Harman security but his rather explosive personality didn't work as well as I'd hoped in that context. That's not Mark's fault," he threw a quick glance his way, "I asked him to profile the company directors and accountants whereas he should just have been making friends with the guys who do the patrols and sit on the desk. He is a man of action and what I needed was more of a sleeper - someone that says and does nothing but sees everything."

"Fortunately I learned a long time ago to have a backup strategy or contingency for everything. You should always have two ways of closing a circuit. In that sense Suzanne was backup for Janet in case anything happened to her. Well something did happen to her. We thought it was a breakdown but it wasn't. While I was waiting in the coffee shop I dialled into a messaging app that I had set up with another member of the same security team that I've only just recruited. Well, I say recruited. I'm not sure I'd put it that way. He certainly wouldn't. It was more of a casual favour but I was hoping he could be developed into a more covert sleeper. He was told not to contact me at all but just to observe. He asked what he should do if he felt that somebody's life was in danger. I assured him that would never be the case but as a backstop (always have a backstop) I had him download a routine, but secure, messaging app.

Anyway he did break cover.

Yesterday.

He sent me a message which was brief and when unencrypted from the app reads:

SSAFEJNOTHARM.

Tell me if you think differently but I interpret that as Suzanne is safe and Janet not harmed. Plus I think I know where they are going. I've booked a flight and it's time now" Hugh said looking at his watch, "for us to go to the airport. "

Chapter Twenty One

As we abandoned the hire car and boarded the plane from Glasgow back to Birmingham I couldn't help thinking about that message. I didn't say anything at the time but I would have said S and J both safe, something like S&JSAFE for example. I mentioned this to Hugh as we sat side by side on the plane – Mark wasn't speaking to him for some reason and Doug stayed in Glasgow after giving us a lift and a surprisingly emotional hug and goodbye in the airport drop off zone.

"I see what you mean but I don't think my source is that precise. Also we had a pre-arranged code for SSAFE being to meet at what we called Suzanne's safe house. Although the text wasn't that exactly it could be either or both of those things, that Suzanne was safe and on the way to the safe location. Anyway that's where we're headed and that's where I think Suzanne will be, and hopefully Janet."

I asked him, but he wouldn't tell me who the source was.

The journey passed extremely slowly. There was a delay while we sat on the plane at Glasgow, before takeoff, waiting for the fog, which had been forecast, to clear and it seemed to take an age when we were back in Solihull and looking for our baggage. More than once we wished we'd just taken hand luggage but Hugh insisted on bringing his mother's battered leather suitcase. It was big enough for a body or three to be concealed in.

Then it was the third taxi that would actually take us all and as far as we wanted to go. What is it about city taxi drivers that they are on some kind of restricted circuit in the city? If you ask them to take you anywhere further it's like you've asked them to cross the Mexican border with a handcart of drugs and all your most distant cousins hanging off the back of a truck.

Tired, sweaty and irritable, we asked the taxi driver to drop us off in the wrong street. I knew where we going. It's was Hugh's Mum's house. Well he could carry his stupid suitcase round the block. Actually Mark did. I asked him if he had forgiven Hugh for not levelling with him about the Harman job. He just grunted. Suit yourself.

After a shower, some beans on toast and some ancient orange cordial, that tasted like car anti-freeze, we felt a lot better. Or at least I did. We still weren't really talking as a group. And now we would wait. Then sleep. Then wait again.

Eventually I was just looking idly out of the bay window at the front of the house when I caught a glimpse of someone I knew. It was one of those bastards in black. I dropped to the floor. Rather theatrically I thought in retrospect and, in a hoarse whisper called out, "Mark, Mark, they're here." Both Hugh and Mark came in. I motioned them to stay back, in the doorway. The guy in black was walking the other way now, not looking at the house. He must have seen me. Damn.

I realised we didn't have a plan for how we were going to deal with this encounter. I asked Hugh. He said he didn't know. He wasn't a man of action. That was Mark's job. Mark said he didn't know, he hadn't got a clue. Great.

Sure enough, a big van passed the house slowly. Then the familiar beeping of a vehicle reversing. It took eight goes to get the back of the van into the small driveway, knocking a small concrete flat stone or plinth off the brick column on one side. The driver wasn't careless. It was just too tight a turn.

We could hear some swearing as the doors opened. Hugh and Mark couldn't see where they were from. But I saw Janet. I saw Janet get out ahead of the rest of them. Then one of the men grabbed her casually around the waist. She pushed him off with a smile and then replaced his arms, on her, around her neck. The driver got out and then another of the guards emerged with his arm around Suzanne's neck and both of her arms behind her back – presumably restrained at the wrist. They marched them to the side door where I knew there was a key under a flower pot. We heard the side door slowly open.

Mark whispered to Hugh, "Now would be a really good time to tell me who your inside man is."

"Ben."

"Ken?"

"Ben." But Mark didn't wait for the clarification. He was off and attacking all three security guards simultaneously. Given the number of people now crowded in and around Hugh's Mum's kitchen this was no mean feat but also, because they were jammed so close together, inevitable. I waded in too, although, like Mark, I didn't really know where to start. Gradually we paired off. Mark floored the big guy and I think knocked him unconscious. Suzanne erupted like a wild thing and was battering the little guy into submission with a pastry roller in one hand and a bread knife in the other that she had grabbed off the side unit. Clearly she hadn't been tied after all. I went to take a swing at the one holding Janet but something in the look of fear and recognition that came from him made me change the angle of attack at the last moment and inadvertently catch Janet square on the jaw. She went down, stunned. The guy just stood facing me. I had recognised him from Harman's. "Ben?"

"Ben," was the answer. We just stood there whilst the rest were seemingly fighting for their lives. Mark had subdued the big guy again (who had only been stunned the first time but now did appear unconscious or worse) and was now looking for more mischief. I stooped down and pulled Suzanne off the little guy. He was finished. You could see the fight had gone out of him. It had from Suzanne as well. When she saw me the red mist cleared and she held me really tightly and then sobbed on to my shoulder. Hugh knelt concernedly by Janet. He was checking her pulse and making sure she was alright. He tried to get her on her side into the classic recovery position but she just groaned and resisted him.

"Better tie her up," I said.

"I've got some handcuffs. Here," said Ben and offered them to Hugh. "I took them off Suzanne".

"What?" said Hugh, still trying to comfort and cradle her. He was trying to bring her round but she was now muttering some curses both at me and Hugh.

I grabbed the handcuffs off Ben, as Hugh was clearly not going to. I rough-housed Janet on to her front, cuffed one wrist and tried to pull the other behind her back. She yelped. Hugh tried to stop me. I was so tempted to hit him too. So tempted.

In the end I just glared at him and yanked Janet's arm all the harder. Once she was double cuffed I stood up, panting in my exertion, head down, staring at the floor. I was deliberately not looking at any of the others, although I could sense them all looking at me; even the Little Canary was open mouthed but not inclined to sing.

Suzanne reattached herself to me now, hugging my right arm tightly. "You knew," she said.

"I didn't, but I suspected."

"Me too," Suzanne replied. "But I didn't want to know, I wanted to believe. I wanted to play the game. We were so strong together."

Ben and Hugh were still looking one to the other as if trying to adjust to our new roles. It was Janet who stepped in. "Your problem, Hugh, is you can analyse people but you have no gut instinct. By which I mean no intuition at an emotional level. You are still a child, expecting all adults to play nicely. Well I've got a shock for you, pal. They don't."

"That's not fair," Suzanne said, "you could say just the same about me."

"True," Janet confirmed.

It was Mark, in his blunt style, who asked the inevitable, "Will someone tell me what the fuck just happened?"

There was a pause then Ben asked, "Hugh, you got my message?"

"Yes," he said, "and I understand it now."

"What message?" Suzanne asked.

Mark and I spoke more or less simultaneously, in time with each other, "Suzanne safe; Janet not Harman."

Hugh groaned, "Yes… Janet hired the security guys. They were working in a freelance capacity, moonlighting from their parent company. We never would have been able to geo-track the van or use any company information to track them down because they weren't working for the company."

Ben looked crestfallen. "In fairness to the guys we all thought Janet was really in danger, because of the gun, but Janet told us to forget the gun but keep Suzanne locked up."

"What gun?" we almost said in unison.

Suzanne just said, "Ah. My bad."

There was a silent pause. It felt like a long time but it was probably just seconds.

"So," I said, trying to summarise, "the big bad company were never guilty of anything? You've made me blow my career for nothing."

Hugh said, "I wouldn't say that. Either of those things. At best Harman & Co. are amoral. They were simply greedy, and afraid of legal complication, rather than evil and manipulative. That probably doesn't make them different from any other commercial company. It was Janet's greed rather than corporate or government responsibility that led first her, then Suzanne, to lose touch with reality."

"So is there a cure, Doctor Hugh?" Suzanne asked.

"No." was the blunt answer. "Janet could probably tell you better than I. As far as I understand it, the experiences are as good as real so the path away is going to be a long and partial one. Like any deep or traumatic experience that alters your personality, it's more a question of taking control and coming to terms with it rather than forgetting."

"But," I asked, "I thought you said Janet had already lost the ability that this game produced and transferred it to Suzanne?"

"That's the part, frankly, I still don't fully understand and I want to spend some time with Janet to study. I suspect that if you took it away from the commercial application you could find something really useful. You could even gamify it in a medical context. Now that would be useful, but it would take a long time. Clinical trials, academic papers, all that."

The look of anger and disgust on Janet's face meant that would probably be a long conversation to even consider it.

"So Janet," I had been dying to ask, "the journal." It sounded like a question but it wasn't. She said nothing. So I asked her something specific.

"Who is Rex and where are you now?"

"Oh Rex. That was just my little joke. We had a guy at work called Rex. He was just an accountant really. Not into the creative side of the game. He wanted in – tried the VR device, used the chemical and physical prep and nothing. Just nothing. He couldn't get it. That was the killer. Project over. If the money men couldn't get it, they refused to fund it. But the truth of it was just that Rex was a giant pain in the ass with zero vision and imagination. He reviewed all the code, line by line, and after several hours his only comment was, "I don't like the colours, they are too bright. What's the big red button for?" As a coding joke we'd put in this big red button on the instructions when you start the game which said, "Don't press me". If you press it the game just ends."

She continued, "I told Rex that you have to 'fake it to make it', using an office cliché of the time, by which I meant you have to be willing to play the game for it to work. It's no different from dungeons and dragons or using a Ouija board. At some level you have to suspend disbelief and just let your mind wander. If you can live it, that's enough to encourage others to suspend their disbelief and for it to become the new reality. That's what the journal is about. I had this character, who

I thought of as a kind of mutant hybrid between Carmen Miranda, Carmen Sandiego and Phe, that would get on a plane and go to random places to sing. It was just a way of kicking it off in my mind. I tried to write it down. But Rex took it all so literally and insisted we manufacture physical props that we could slip in like fake airline tickets and the like. But that would limit the options unnecessarily. What I experienced was more random giving an infinite kaleidoscope of options that you could never exhaust as no two games would be the same. You select a button, open a door, go through a portal, whatever is appropriate to the scenario you're in and a unique adventure starts. So I guess that 'Rex me fecit' was my pathetic little pun about Rex. Rex made me (what I am). In my view he forced me to take the game home and develop it myself, but it was also a joke against him and ultimately me. I had to fake it to try and make it. But I couldn't fake it anymore – the system just wears off, you grow a tolerance for the drugs, and the novelty of the device, and for me it just faded out. The more familiar I got with it the more my conscious mind took over. Like waking up from a dream just when it's getting interesting."

Hugh started rattling on about some guy called Alfred Adler, who had split up with Freud, but I don't think we were listening. I did hear him say he could offer Janet a potential solution through dream therapy, guided meditation and hypnosis and that he was prepared to use this in exchange for some kind of plea-bargaining with the authorities.

Now I came to think about it I couldn't work out who would get charged with what criminal offences. Imprisonment, actual bodily harm, reckless endangerment, damage to property. I reckon we'd all get done for something. Perhaps we'd be better keeping quiet and starting a mutual therapy group! I suggested that to them adding, rather sarcastically, "but it might mean Janet has to abandon her ambitions for global domination and her evil empire."

Hugh warned, "you shouldn't joke about or underestimate the pain of psychological therapy and re-conditioning that some people undergo. Nonetheless I'm warming to the idea of working further on this with Janet. We should do it in pairs, at least initially."

"Great", said Mark, "does that mean I get Ben and you get Janet?"

"And," said Ben, "Ken gets Little Canary!"

"Right, and Phe could be rule reader and games-master," concluded Hugh finally seeing the joke and not taking the whole thing too seriously.

Then, after a moment's reflection, he added "you may think I'm emotionally naïve and don't understand Janet at all, but one thing that's obvious to me is that John and Suzanne have some issues that they need to spend more time together to sort out."

Suzanne was still holding on to me and me to her. We looked at each other with a look of what? Recognition? Relief? Hope? Friendship? Whatever it was seemed to surprise us, but not so much the others. We had persisted in being mutually exclusive 'I's in the telling of our story. But 'we' would be more accurate. It was always our story and we could take it forward in any direction, any time, any place.

Author Biography (quite condensed)

Ade Annabel describes himself as 'a carbon based lifeform from somewhere near Goonhilly' which is simply not true. Not the bit about Goonhilly anyway.

He is married, lives in the UK, and has worked in the Arts, Horticulture and Information Technology. He has written articles for a number of newspapers and magazines and in 2018 published his first novel called Dig Pie Eye which was based loosely on a garden makeover in Port Isaac in Cornwall, UK, in which the gardeners accidentally take on the role of slightly inebriated private eyes. A more sober sequel is due for release and is set in Sherwood Forest.

In his spare time Ade enjoys walking, gardening and thinking about home improvements ('I said I'd get it done – there's no point in reminding me every year!')

www.ingramcontent.com/pod-product-compliance
Lightning Source LLC
Chambersburg PA
CBHW032143020726
47496CB00003B/690